BANANA FOX AND THE GUMMY MONSTER MESS

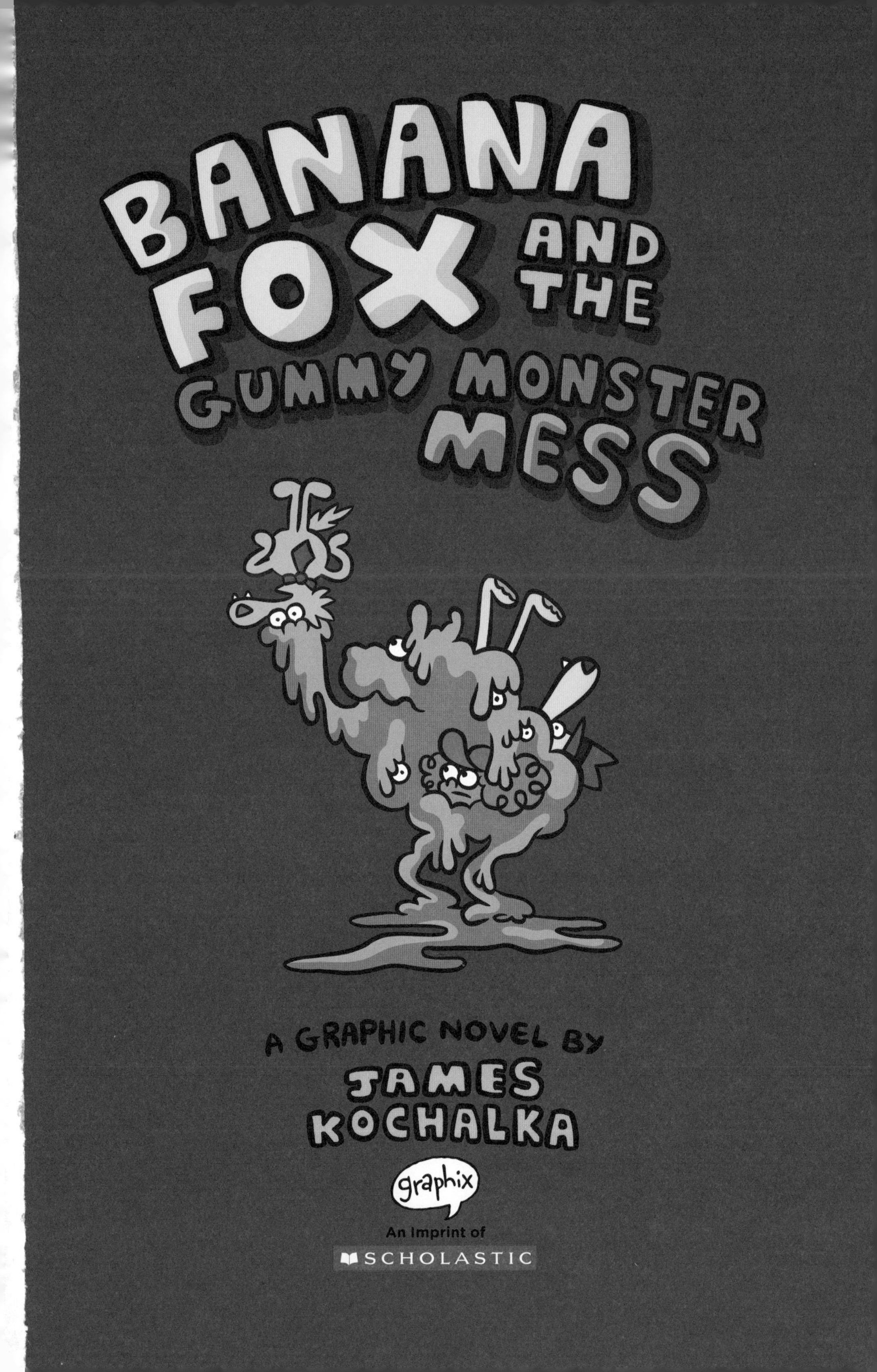

A GRAPHIC NOVEL BY

JAMES KOCHALKA

graphix

An imprint of

SCHOLASTIC

For Aunt Margy

Copyright © 2022 by James Kochalka

All rights reserved. Published by Graphix, an imprint of Scholastic Inc.,
Publishers since 1920. SCHOLASTIC, GRAPHIX, and associated logos are
trademarks and/or registered trademarks of Scholastic Inc.

The publisher does not have any control over and does not assume any
responsibility for author or third-party websites or their content.

No part of this publication may be reproduced, stored in a retrieval
system, or transmitted in any form or by any means, electronic, mechanical,
photocopying, recording, or otherwise, without written permission of the
publisher. For information regarding permission, write to Scholastic Inc.,
Attention: Permissions Department, 557 Broadway, New York, NY 10012.

This book is a work of fiction. Names, characters, places, and incidents
are either the product of the author's imagination or are used fictitiously,
and any resemblance to actual persons, living or dead, business
establishments, events, or locales is entirely coincidental.

Library of Congress Control Number: 2021937767

ISBN 978-1-338-66055-5 (hardcover)
ISBN 978-1-338-66054-8 (paperback)

10 9 8 7 6 5 4 3 2 1   22 23 24 25 26

Printed in China   62
First edition, May 2022

Edited by Megan Peace
Book design by Steve Ponzo
Creative Director: Phil Falco
Publisher: David Saylor

CONTENTS

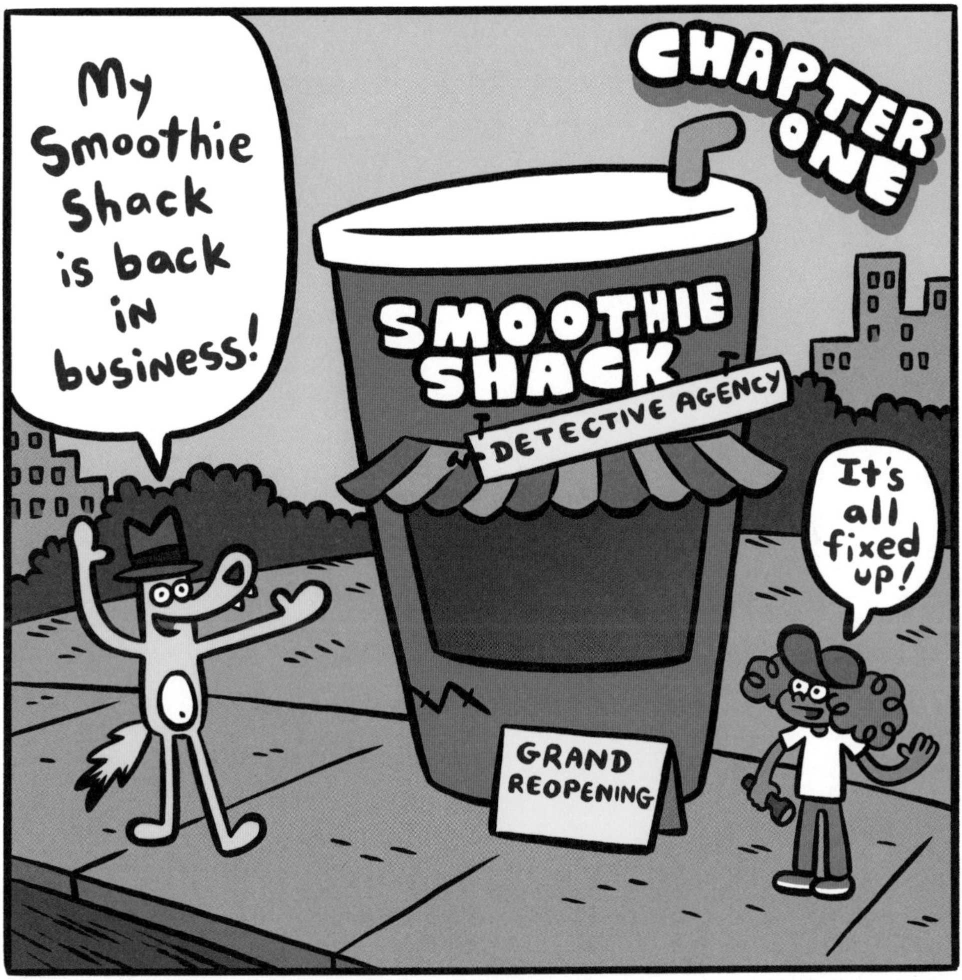
CHAPTER ONE
My Smoothie Shack is back in business!
SMOOTHIE SHACK
DETECTIVE AGENCY
GRAND REOPENING
It's all fixed up!

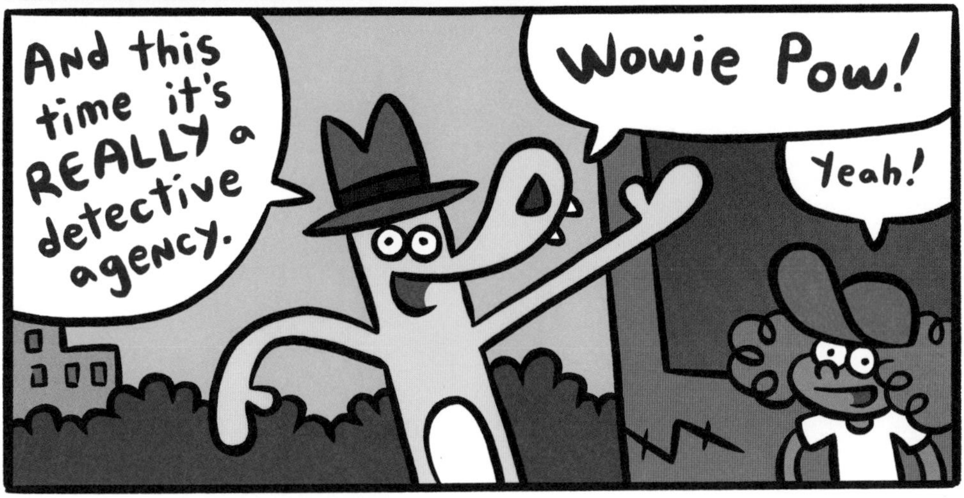
And this time it's REALLY a detective agency.
Wowie Pow!
Yeah!

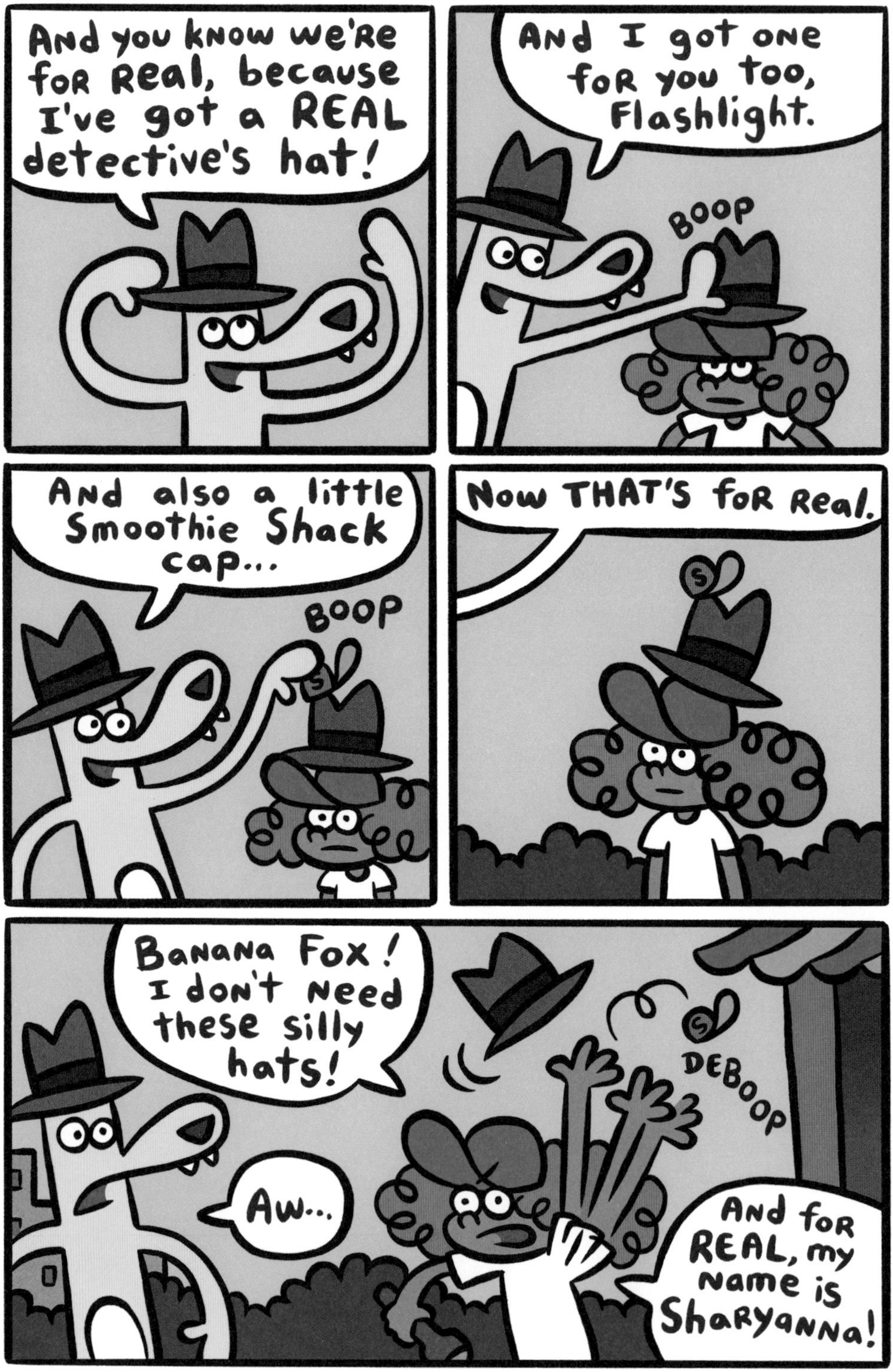
And you know we're for real, because I've got a REAL detective's hat!
And I got one for you too, Flashlight.
BOOP
And also a little Smoothie Shack cap...
BOOP
Now THAT'S for real.
Banana Fox! I don't need these silly hats!
DEBOOP
Aw...
And for REAL, my name is Sharyanna!

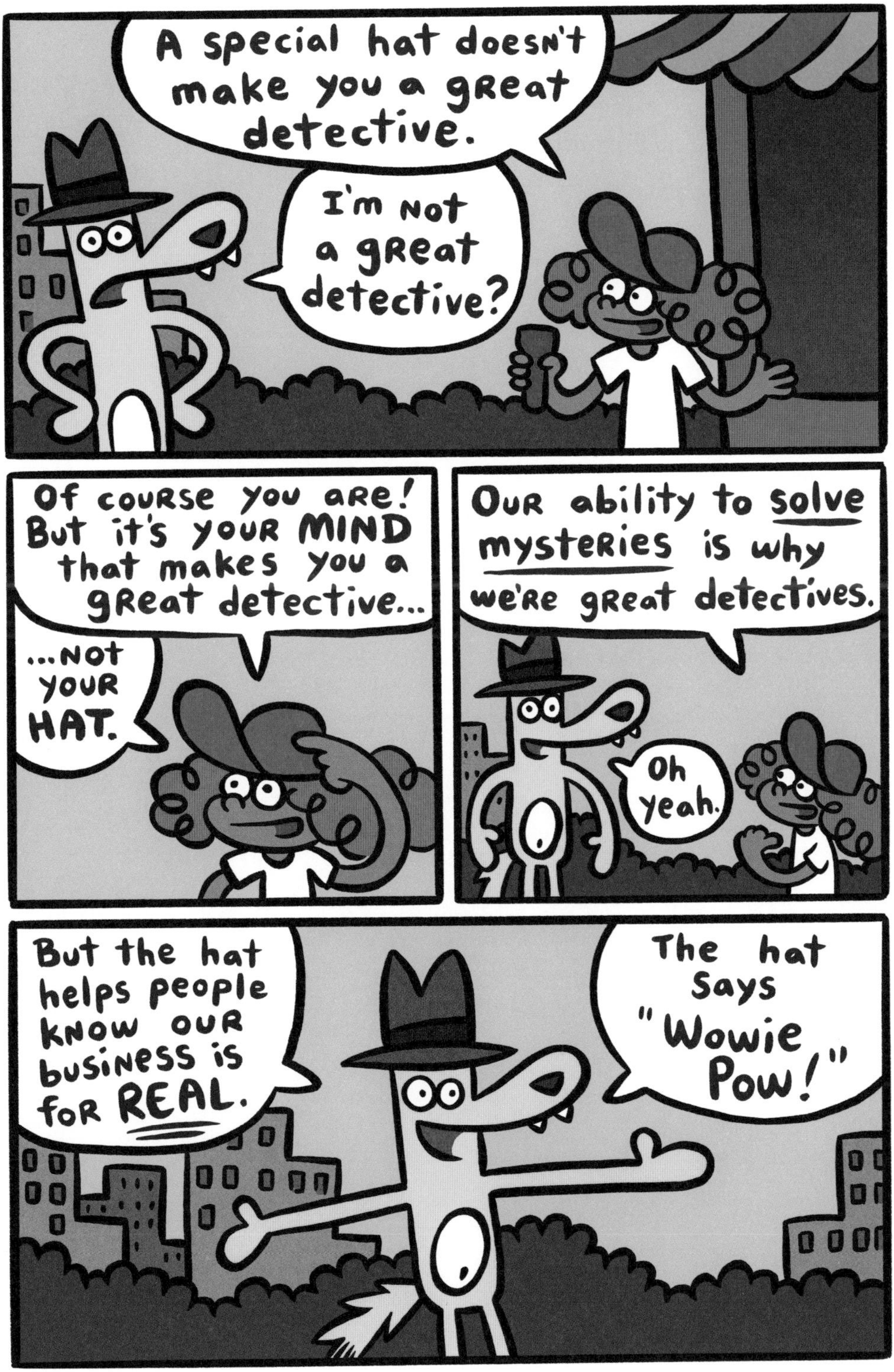
A special hat doesn't make you a great detective.
I'm not a great detective?
Of course you are! But it's your MIND that makes you a great detective...
...not your HAT.
Our ability to solve mysteries is why we're great detectives.
Oh yeah.
But the hat helps people know our business is for REAL.
The hat says "Wowie Pow!"

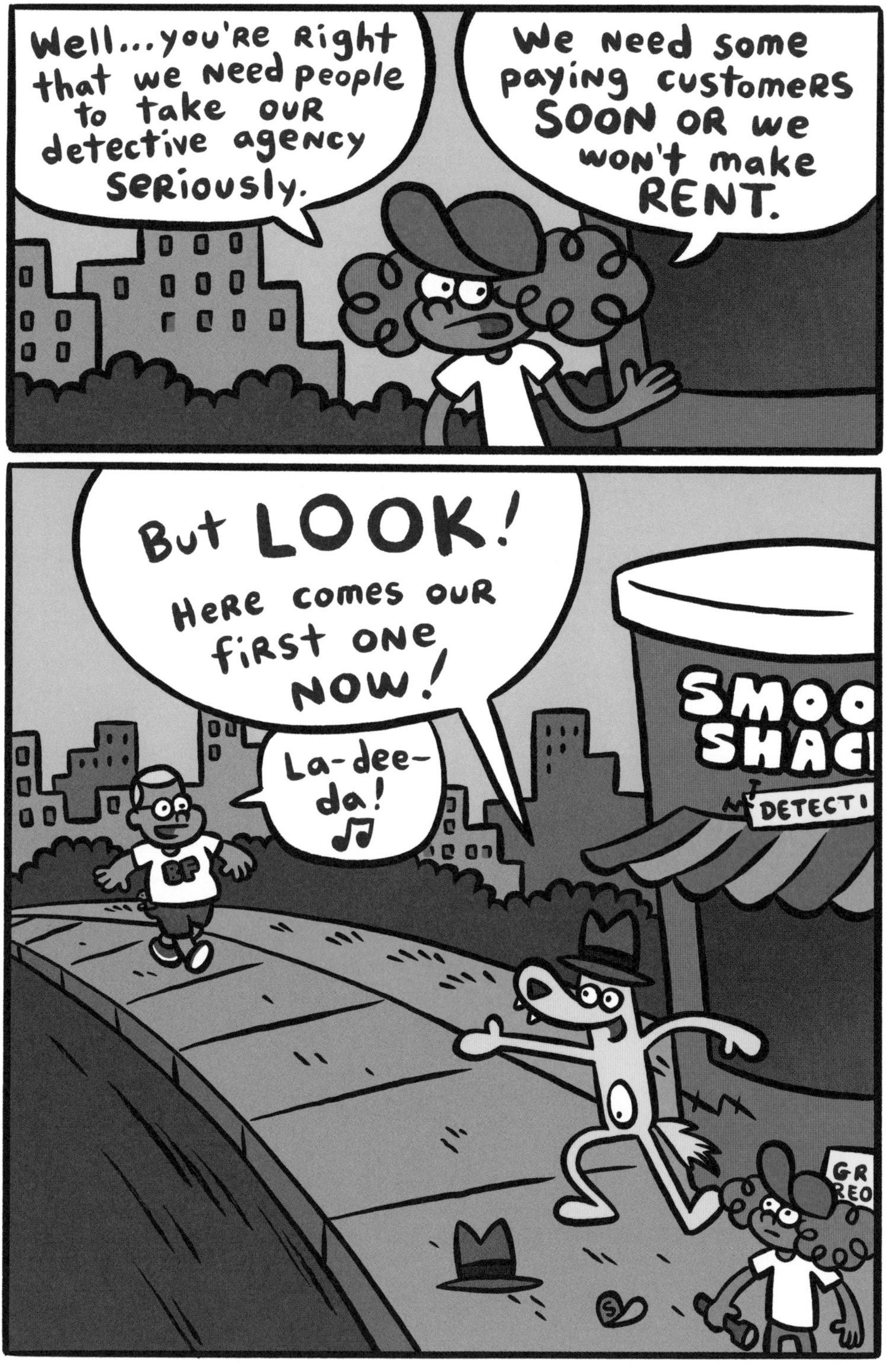
Well...you're right that we need people to take our detective agency seriously.
We need some paying customers SOON OR we won't make RENT.
But LOOK! Here comes our first one NOW!
La-dee-da! ♫
SMOO
SHAC
DETECTI
GR
REO

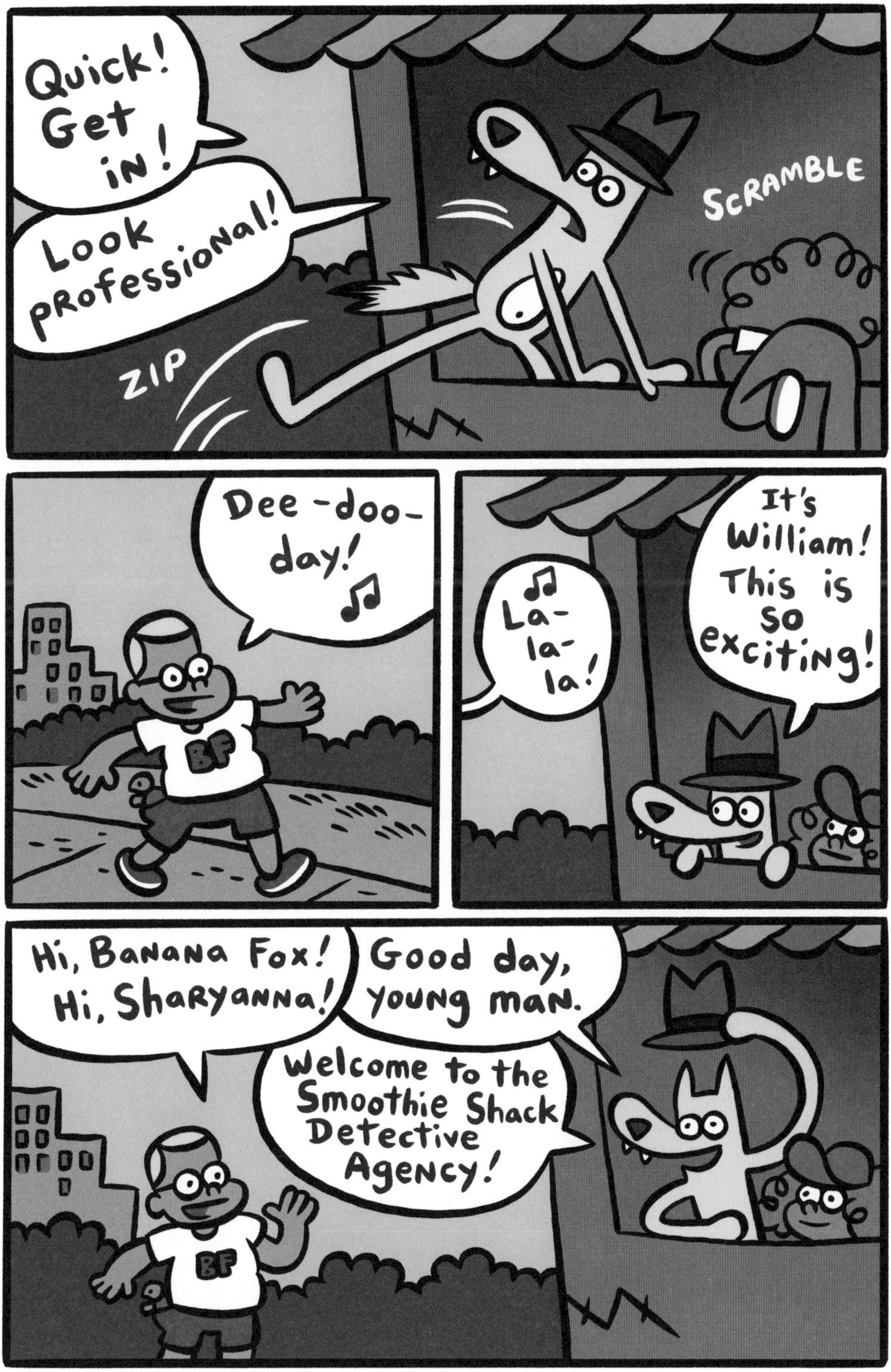
Quick! Get in!
Look professional!
ZIP
SCRAMBLE
Dee-doo-day!
La-la-la!
It's William! This is so exciting!
Hi, Banana Fox! Hi, Sharyanna!
Good day, young man.
Welcome to the Smoothie Shack Detective Agency!

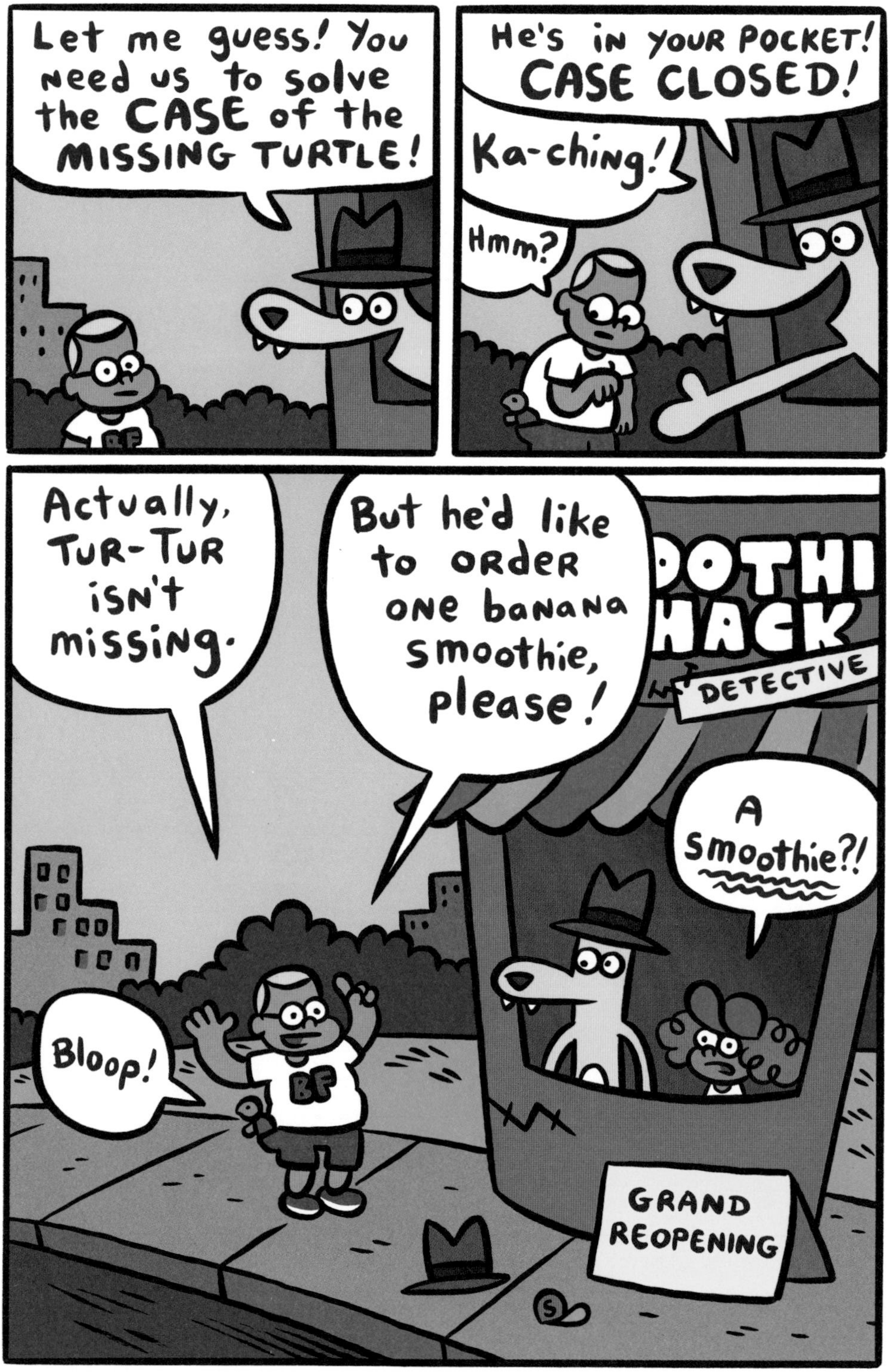

Let me guess! You need us to solve the CASE of the MISSING TURTLE!
He's in your POCKET! CASE CLOSED!
Ka-ching!
Hmm?
Actually, TUR-TUR isn't missing.
But he'd like to order one banana smoothie, please!
DETECTIVE
A smoothie?!
Bloop!
GRAND REOPENING

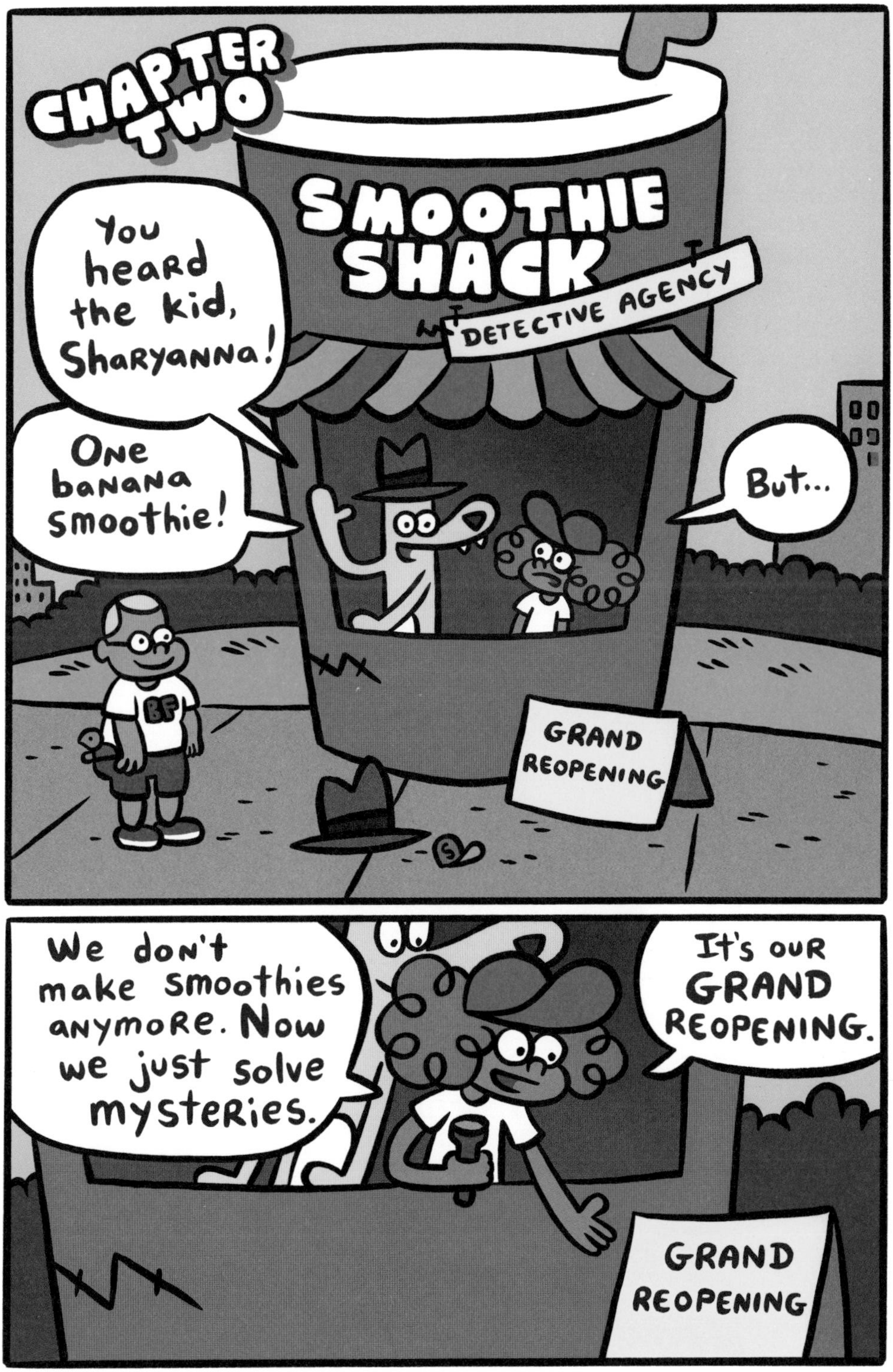
CHAPTER TWO
SMOOTHIE SHACK
DETECTIVE AGENCY
You heard the kid, Sharyanna!
One banana smoothie!
But...
GRAND REOPENING
We don't make smoothies anymore. Now we just solve mysteries.
It's our GRAND REOPENING.
GRAND REOPENING

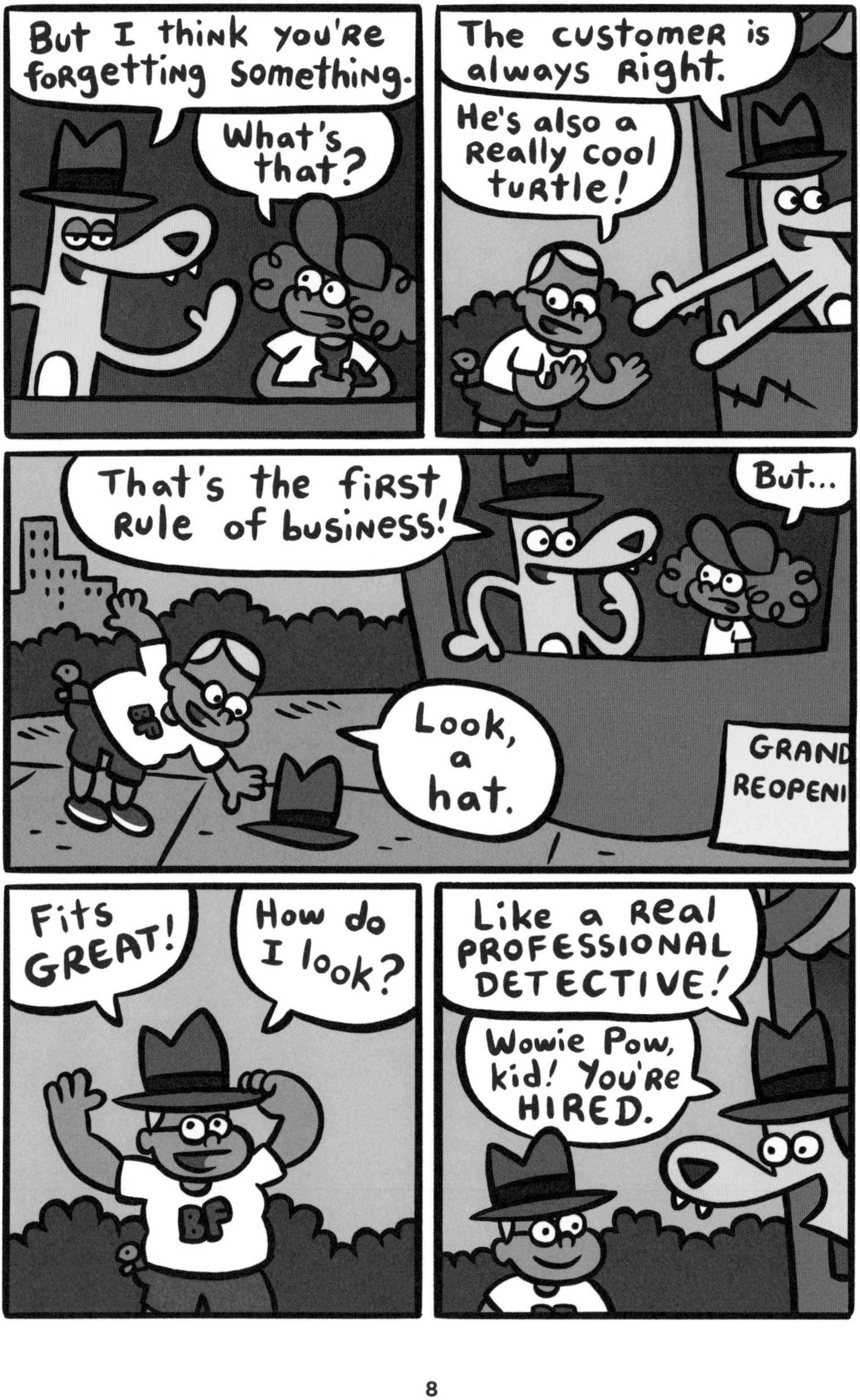

But I think you're forgetting something.
What's that?
The customer is always right.
He's also a really cool turtle!
That's the first rule of business!
But...
Look, a hat.
GRAND
REOPENI
Fits GREAT!
How do I look?
Like a real PROFESSIONAL DETECTIVE!
Wowie Pow, kid! You're HIRED.

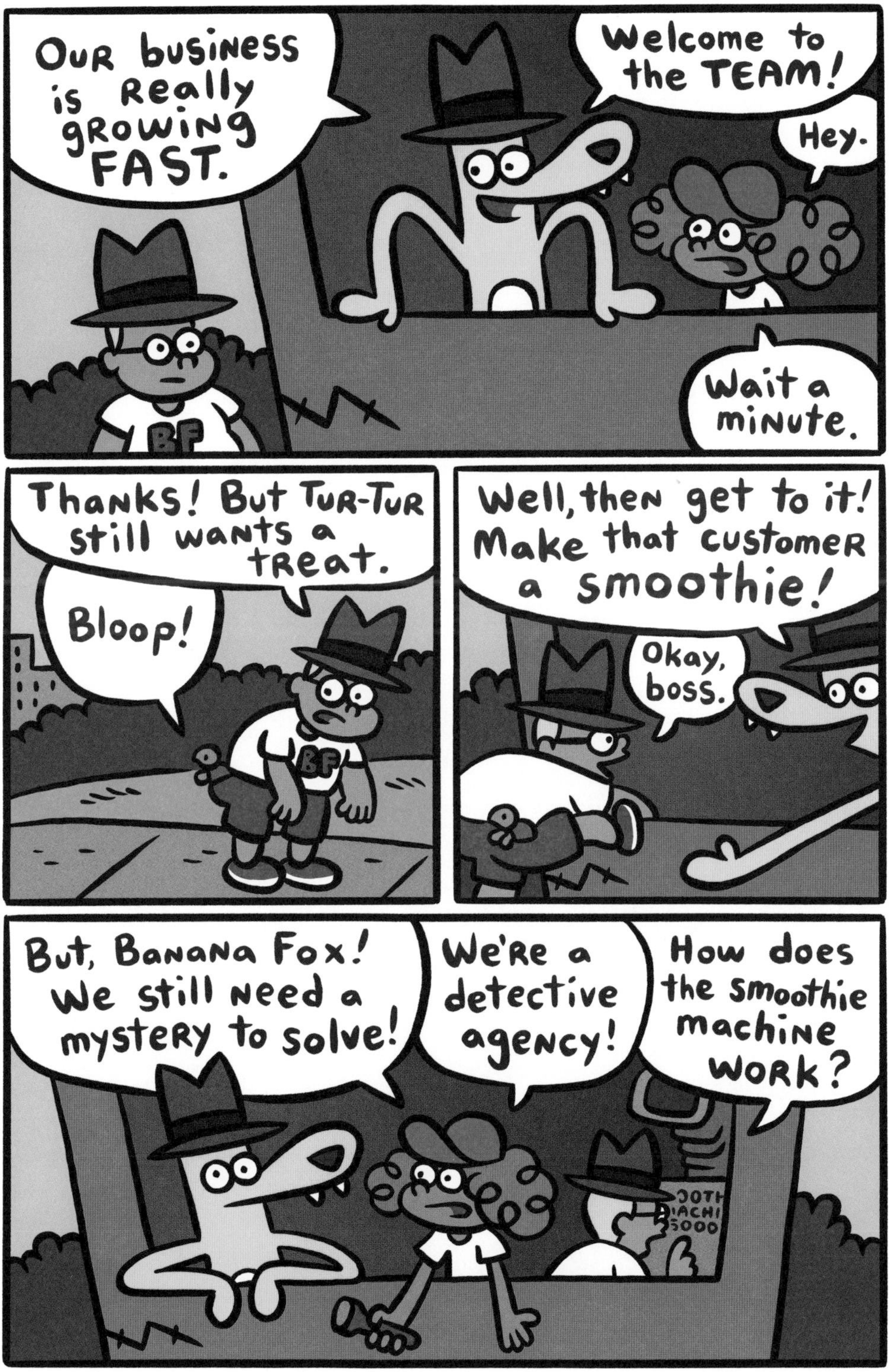
Our business is really growing FAST.
Welcome to the TEAM!
Hey.
Wait a minute.
Thanks! But Tur-Tur still wants a treat.
Bloop!
Well, then get to it! Make that customer a smoothie!
Okay, boss.
But, Banana Fox! We still need a mystery to solve!
We're a detective agency!
How does the smoothie machine work?

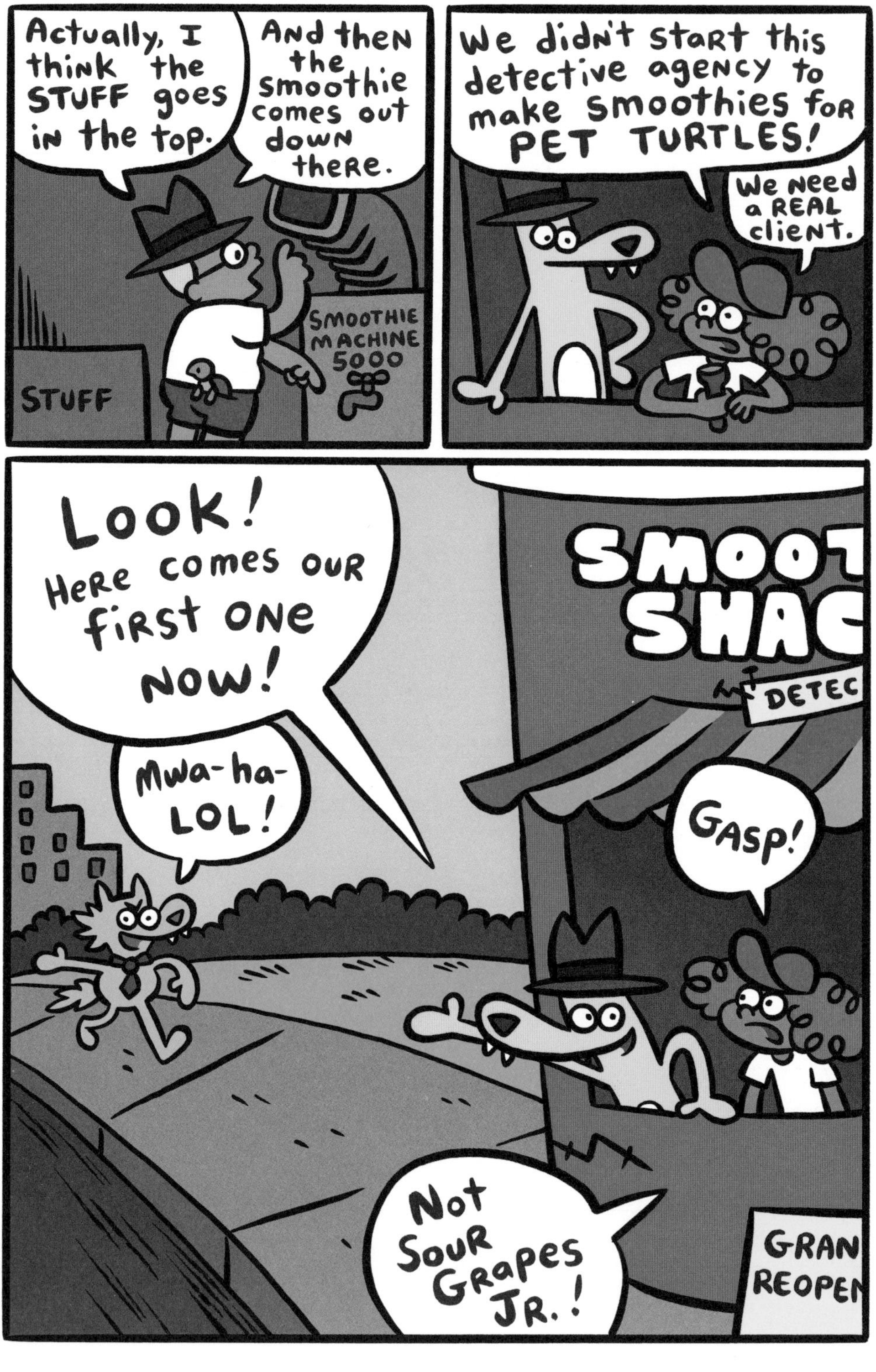
Actually, I think the STUFF goes in the top.
And then the smoothie comes out down there.
STUFF
SMOOTHIE MACHINE 5000
We didn't start this detective agency to make smoothies for PET TURTLES!
We need a REAL client.
LOOK! Here comes our first one now!
Mwa-ha-LOL!
SMOOT
SHAC
DETEC
GASP!
Not Sour Grapes Jr.!
GRAN
REOPEN

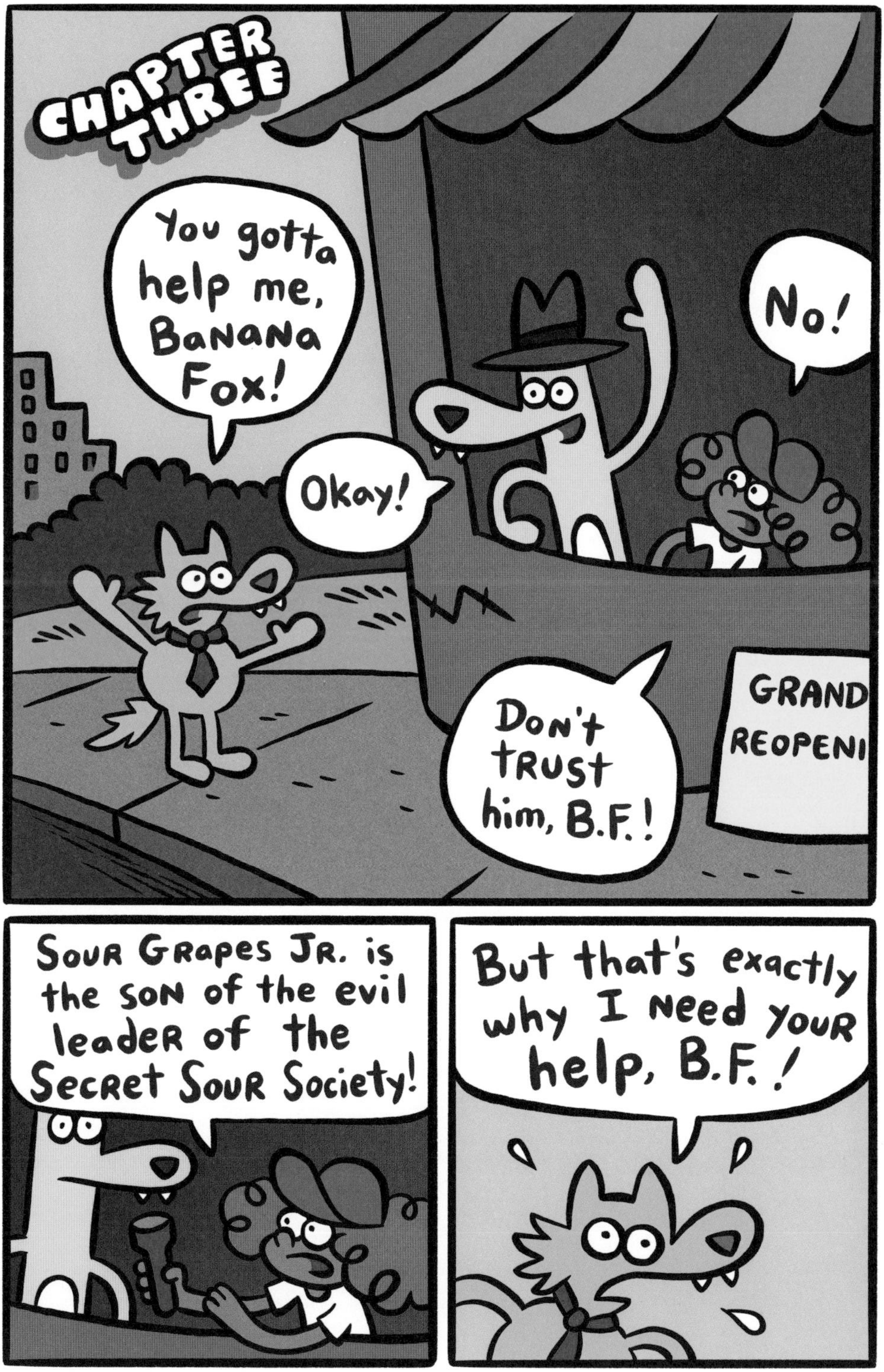
CHAPTER THREE
You gotta help me, Banana Fox!
Okay!
No!
Don't TRUST him, B.F.!
GRAND
REOPENI
Sour Grapes Jr. is the son of the evil leader of the Secret Sour Society!
But that's exactly why I need your help, B.F.!

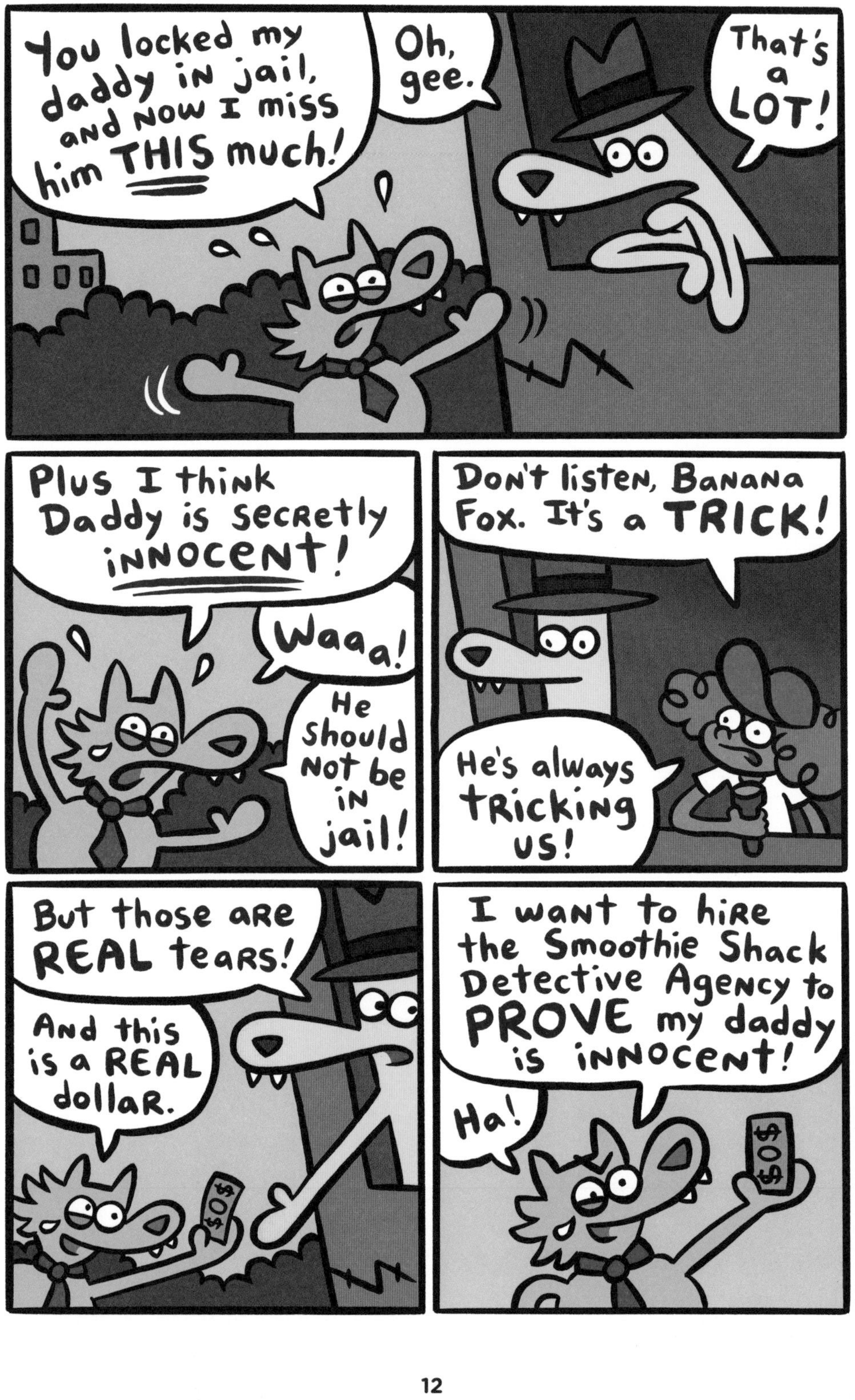
You locked my daddy in jail, and now I miss him THIS much!
Oh, gee.
That's a LOT!
Plus I think Daddy is secretly innocent!
Waaa!
He should not be in jail!
Don't listen, Banana Fox. It's a TRICK!
He's always tricking us!
But those are REAL tears!
And this is a REAL dollar.
I want to hire the Smoothie Shack Detective Agency to PROVE my daddy is innocent!
Ha!

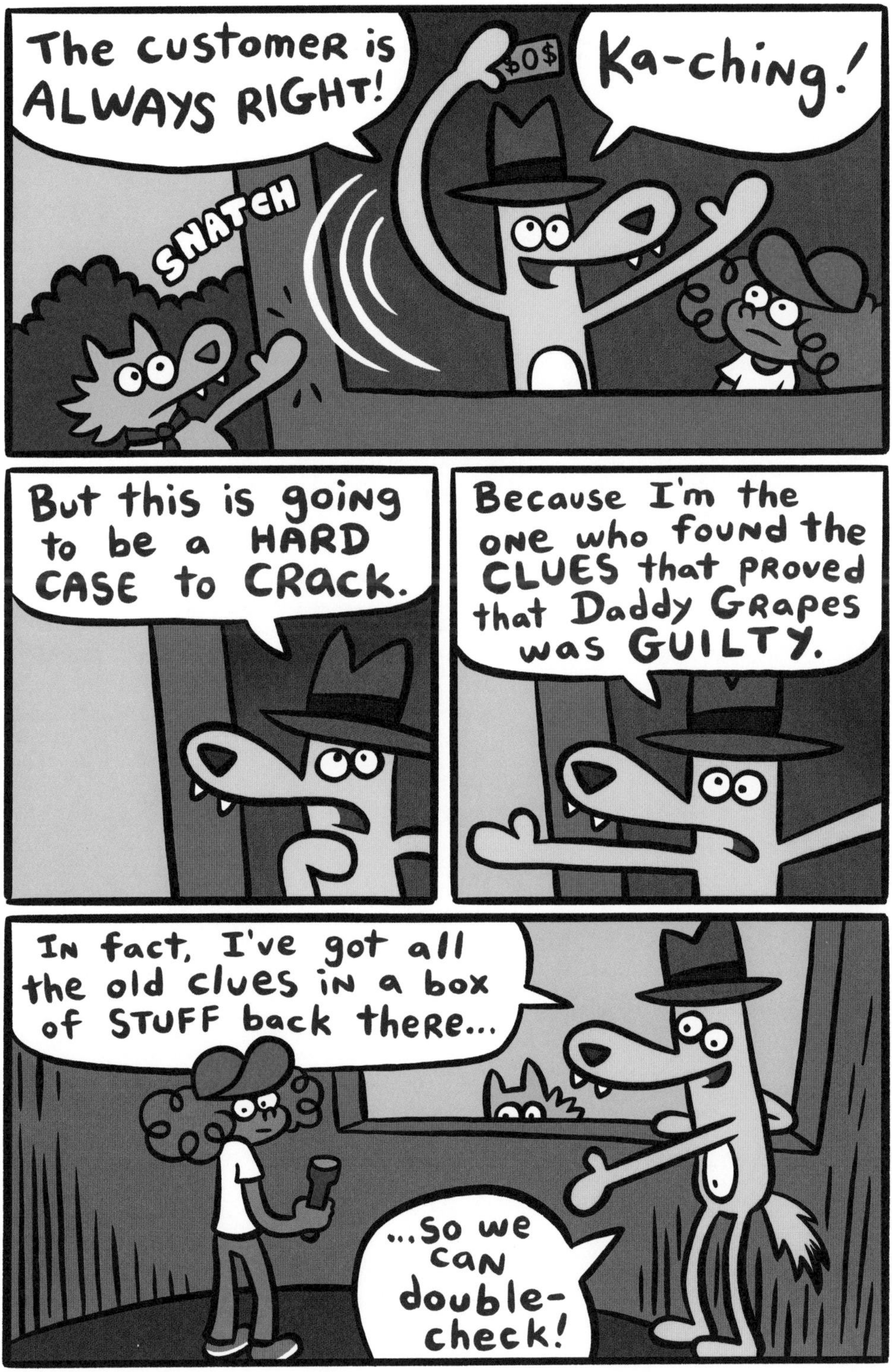
The customer is ALWAYS RIGHT!
0
Ka-ching!
SNATCH
But this is going to be a HARD CASE to CRACK.
Because I'm the one who found the CLUES that proved that Daddy Grapes was GUILTY.
In fact, I've got all the old clues in a box of STUFF back there...
...So we can double-check!

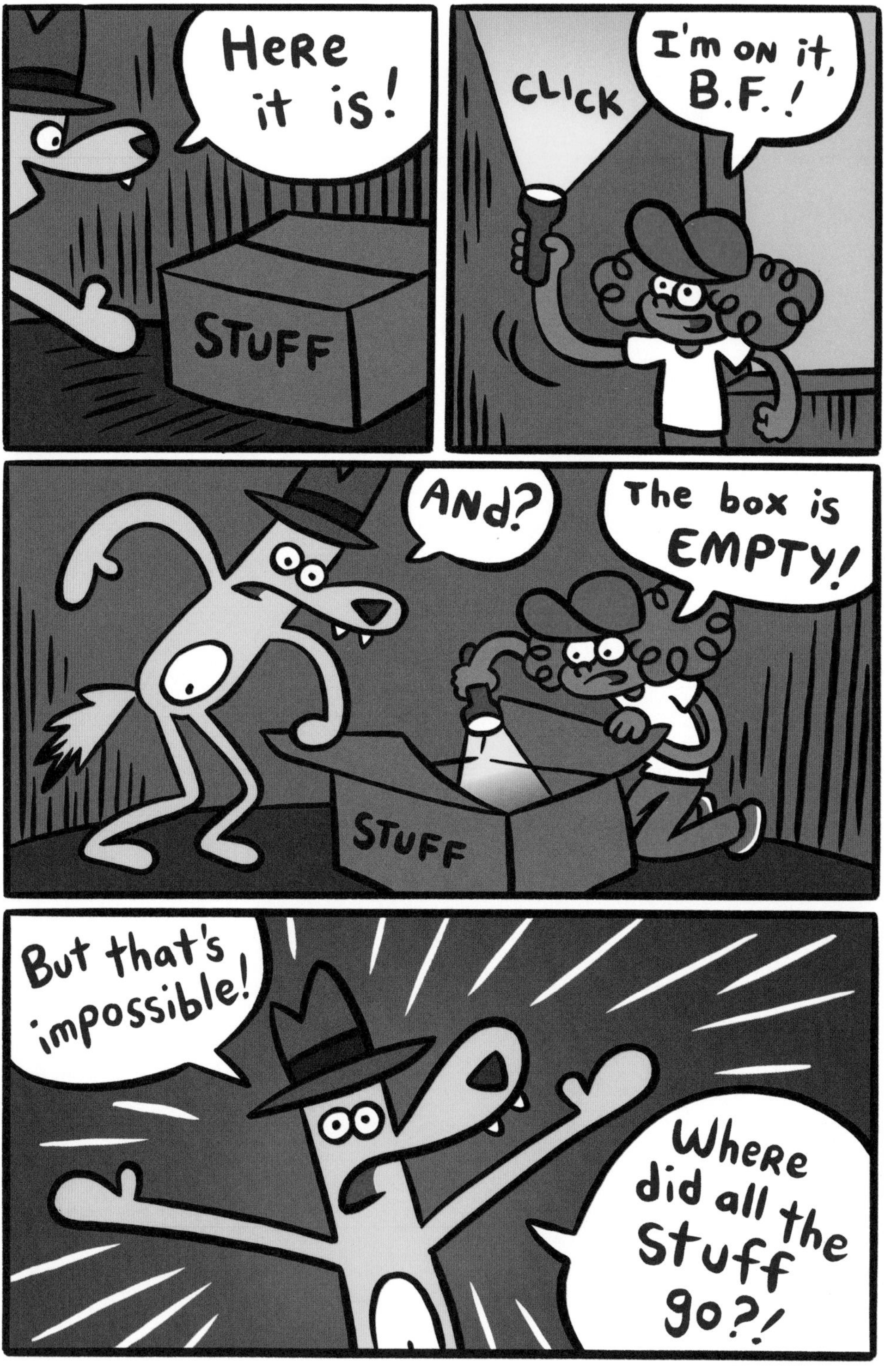
Here it is!
STUFF
CLICK
I'm on it, B.F.!
And?
The box is EMPTY!
STUFF
But that's impossible!
Where did all the Stuff go?!

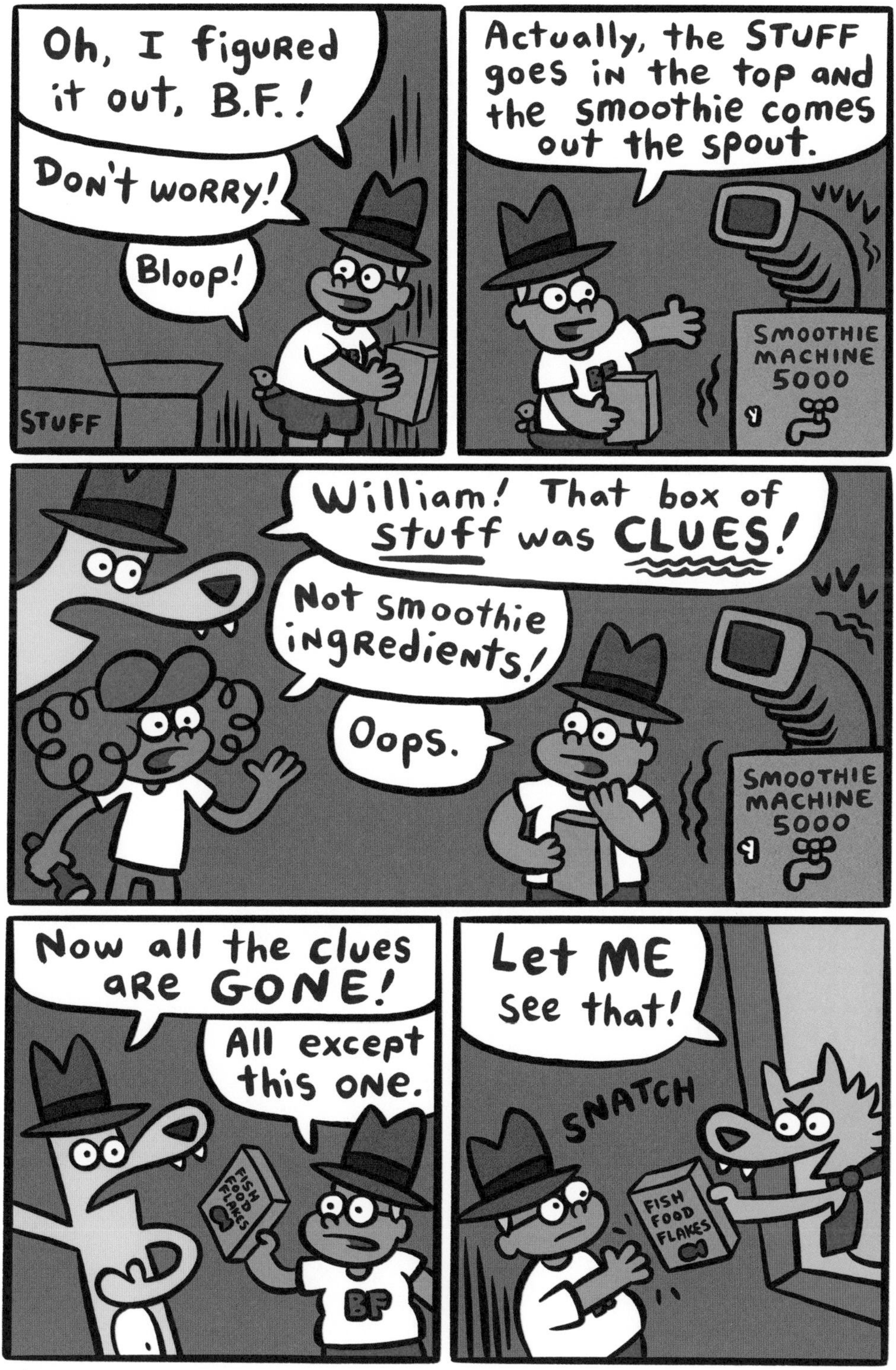
Oh, I figured it out, B.F.!
Don't worry!
Bloop!
STUFF
Actually, the STUFF goes in the top and the smoothie comes out the spout.
SMOOTHIE MACHINE 5000
William! That box of stuff was CLUES!
Not smoothie ingredients!
Oops.
SMOOTHIE MACHINE 5000
Now all the clues are GONE!
All except this one.
FISH FOOD FLAKES
BF
Let ME see that!
SNATCH
FISH FOOD FLAKES

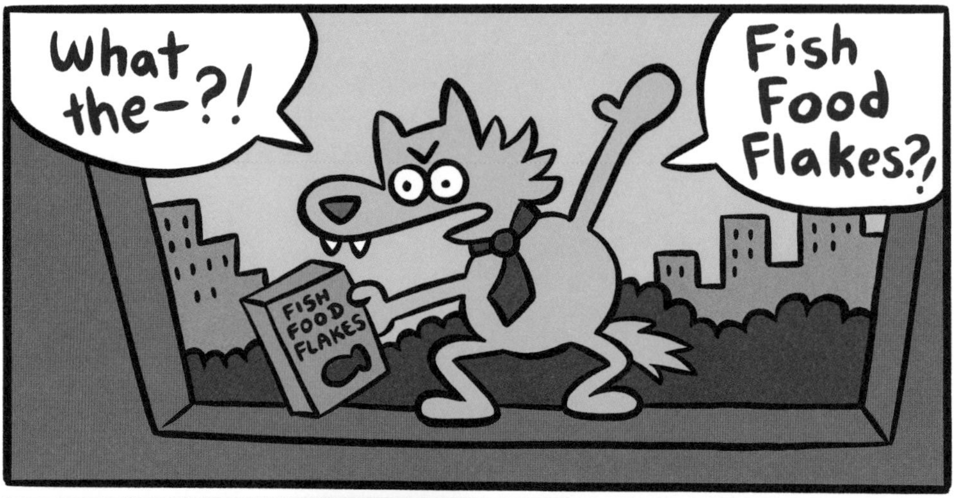
What the-?!
Fish Food Flakes?!
FISH FOOD FLAKES

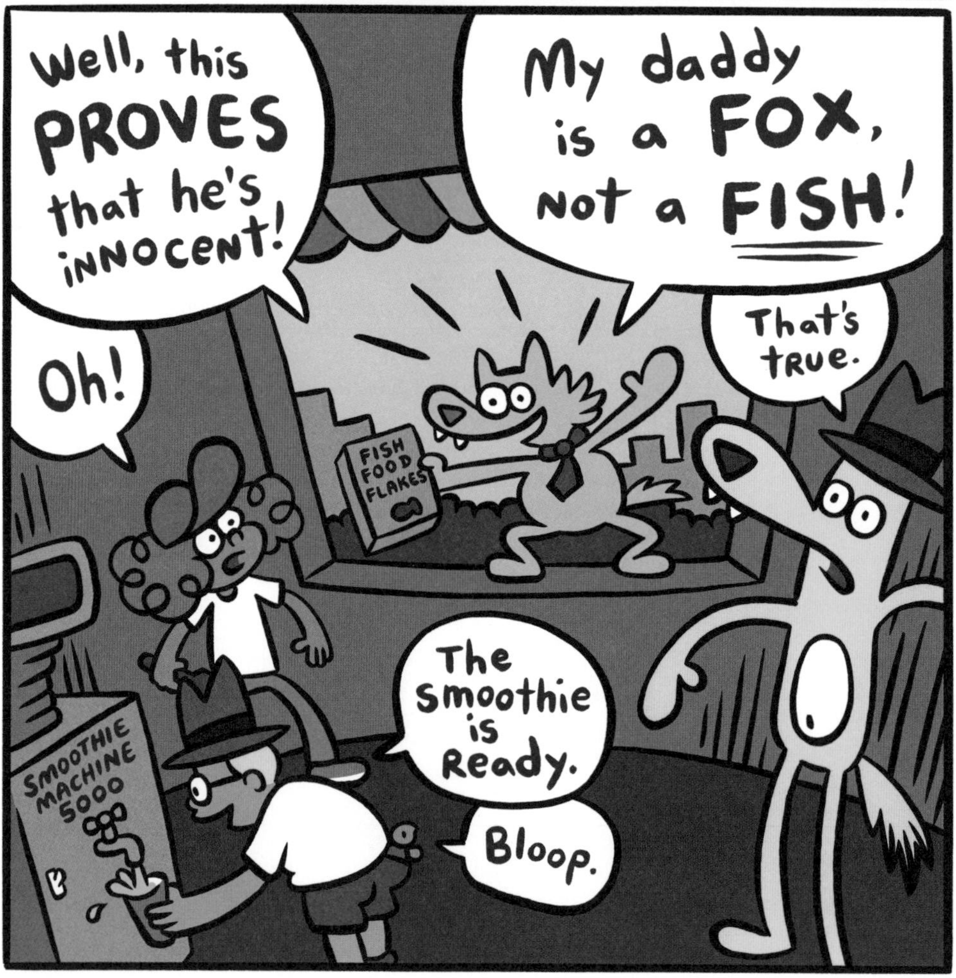
Well, this PROVES that he's innocent!
My daddy is a FOX, not a FISH!
That's true.
Oh!
FISH FOOD FLAKES
The smoothie is Ready.
Bloop.
SMOOTHIE MACHINE 5000

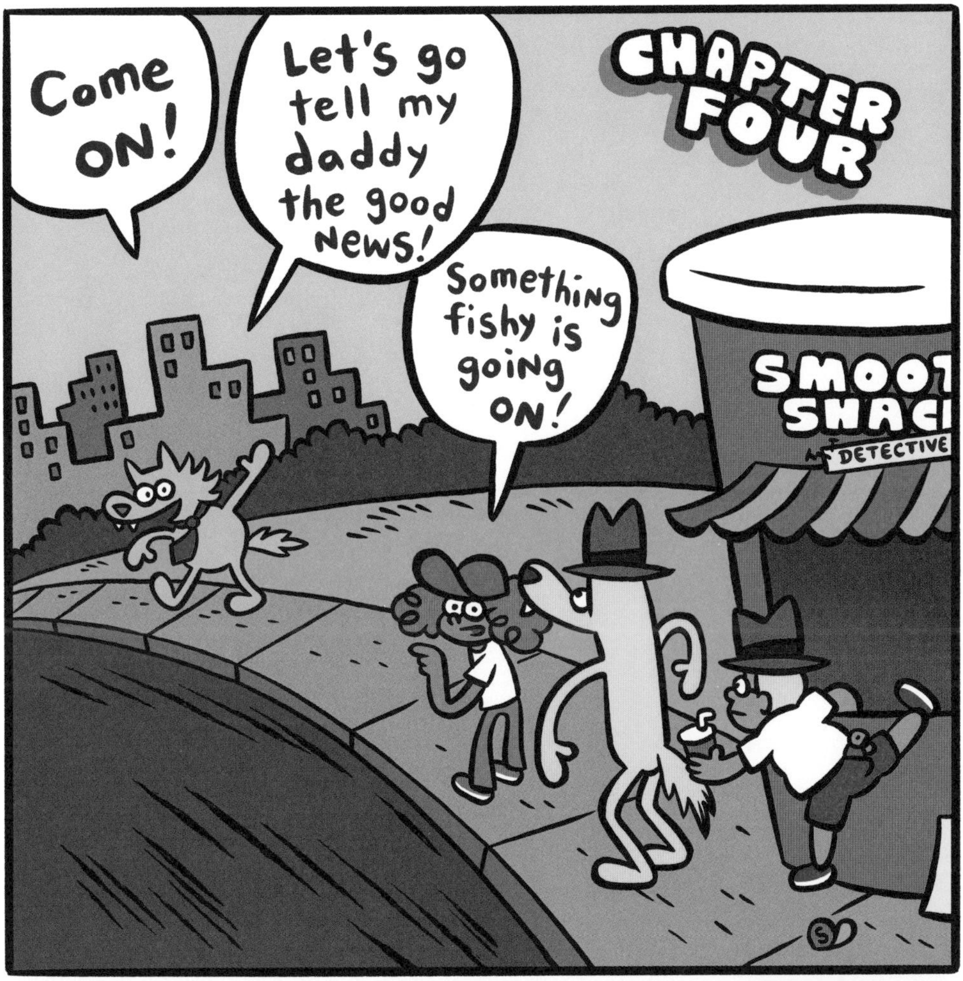
CHAPTER FOUR
Come ON!
Let's go tell my daddy the good NEWS!
Something fishy is going ON!
SMOOT
SHAC
DETECTIVE

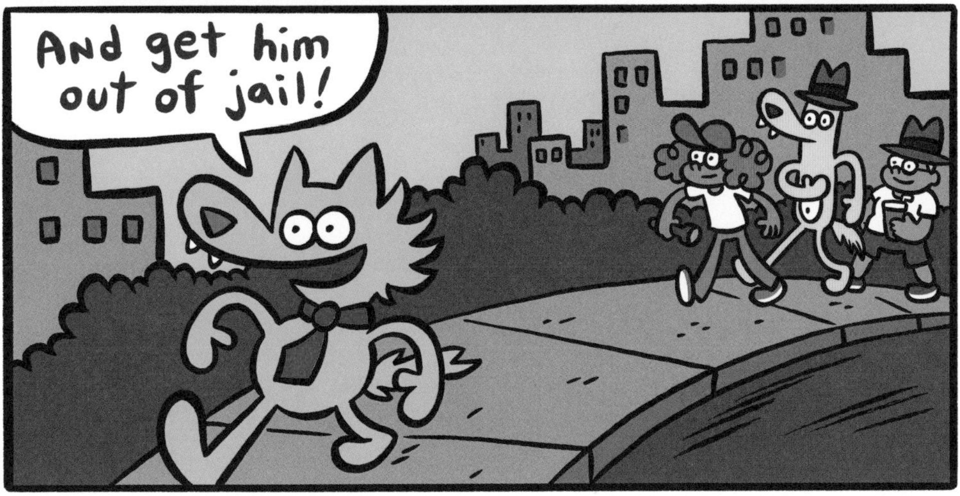
And get him out of jail!

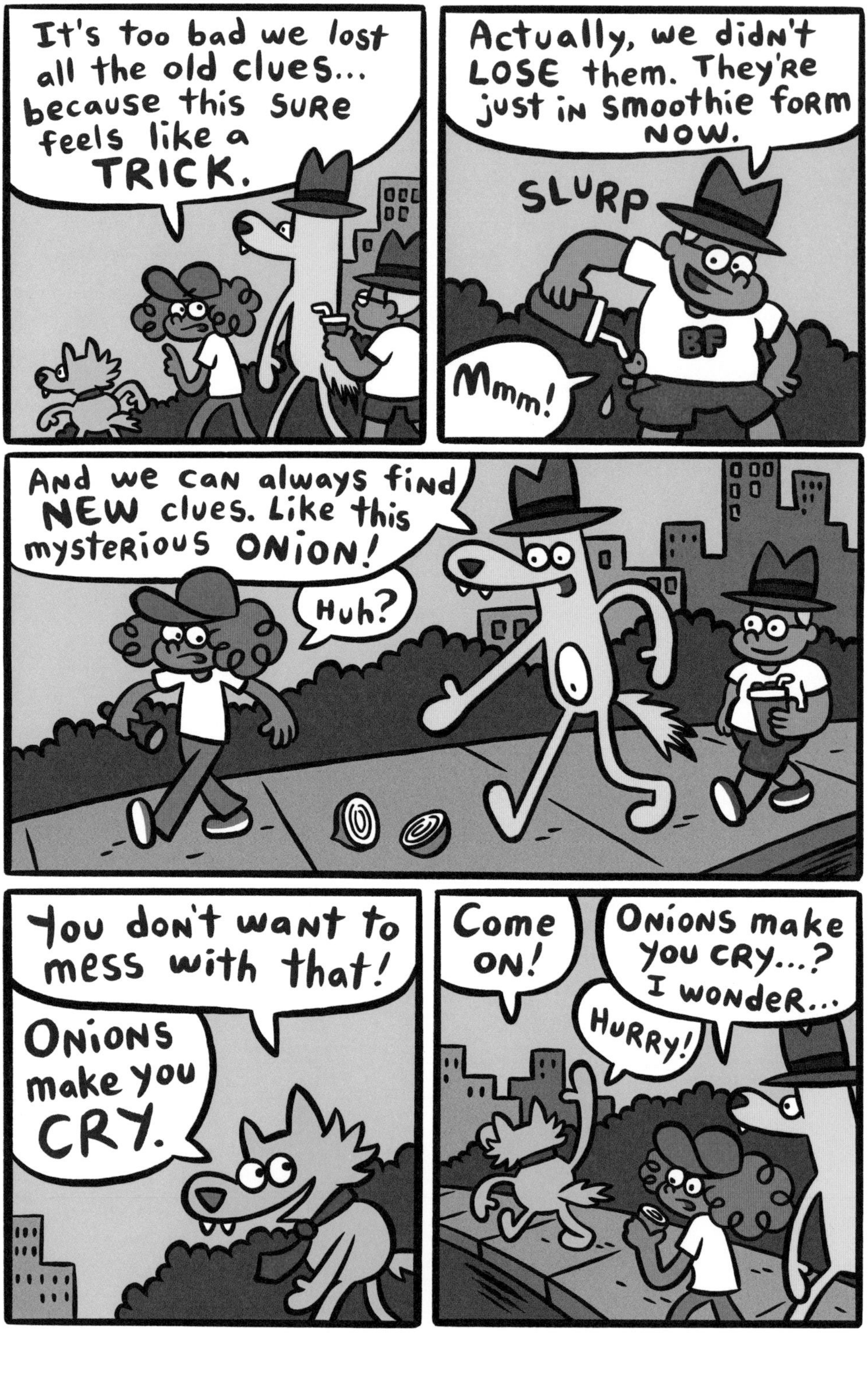
It's too bad we lost all the old clues... because this SURE feels like a TRICK.
Actually, we didn't LOSE them. They're just in smoothie form NOW.
SLURP
BF
Mmm!
And we can always find NEW clues. Like this mysterious ONION!
Huh?
You don't want to mess with that!
ONIONS make you CRY.
Come ON!
ONIONS make you CRY...? I wonder...
HURRY!

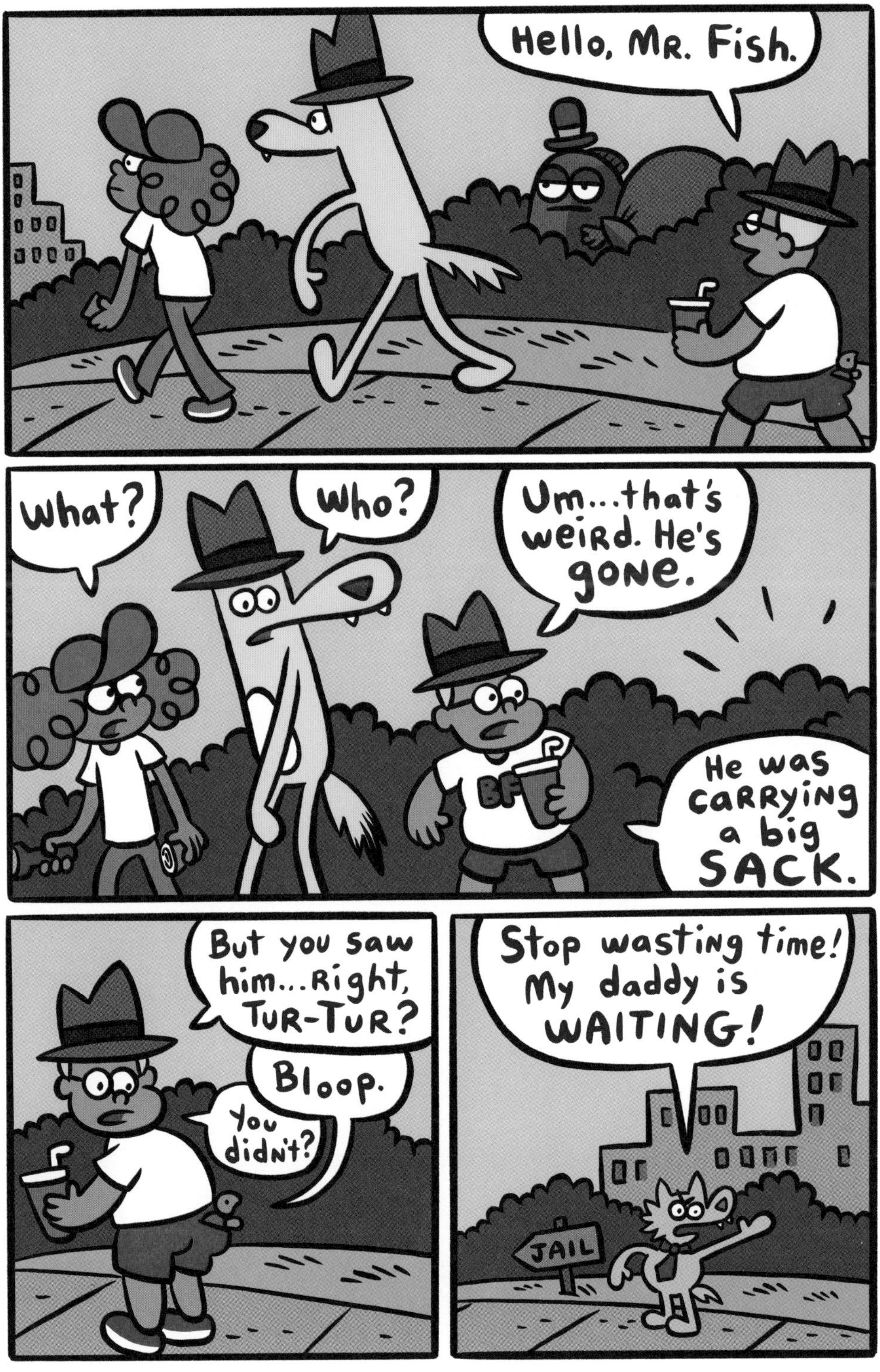
Hello, Mr. Fish.
What?
Who?
Um...that's weird. He's gone.
He was carrying a big SACK.
But you saw him...Right, Tur-Tur?
Bloop.
You didn't?
Stop wasting time! My daddy is WAITING!
JAIL

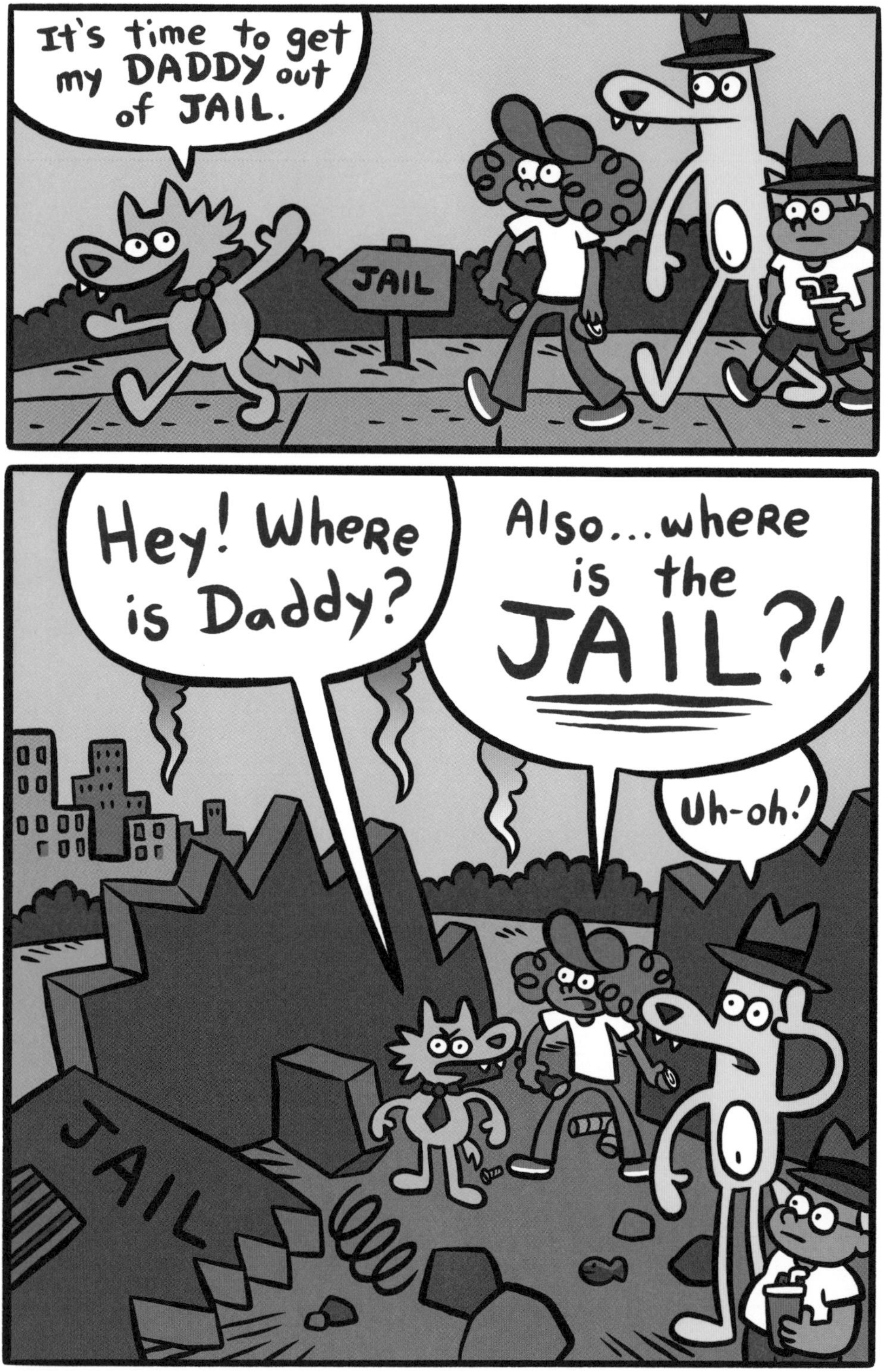
It's time to get my DADDY out of JAIL.
JAIL
Hey! Where is Daddy?
Also...where is the JAIL?!
Uh-oh!
JAIL

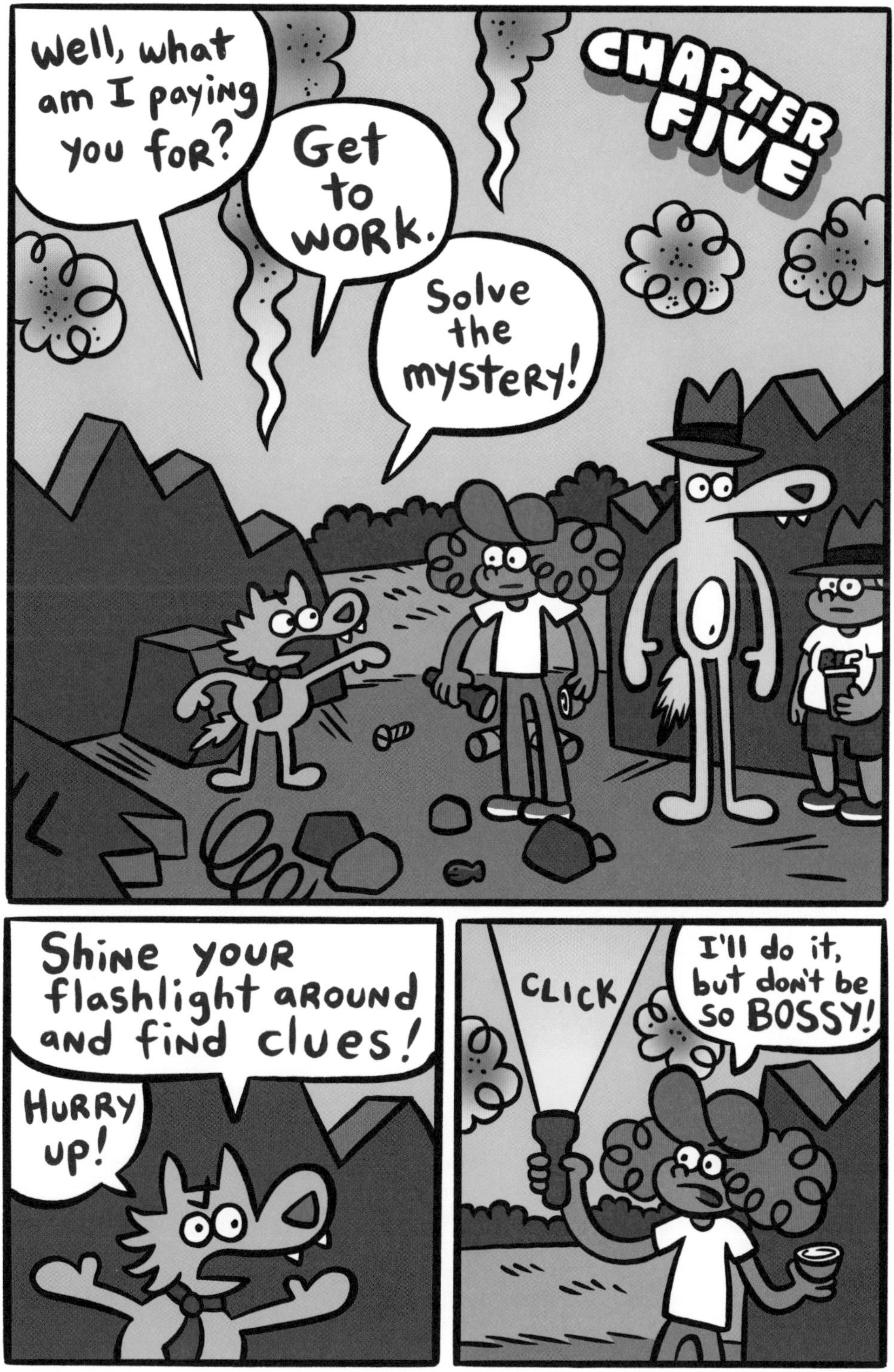
CHAPTER FIVE
Well, what am I paying you for?
Get to WORK.
Solve the mystery!
Shine your flashlight around and find clues!
HURRY up!
CLICK
I'll do it, but don't be so BOSSY!

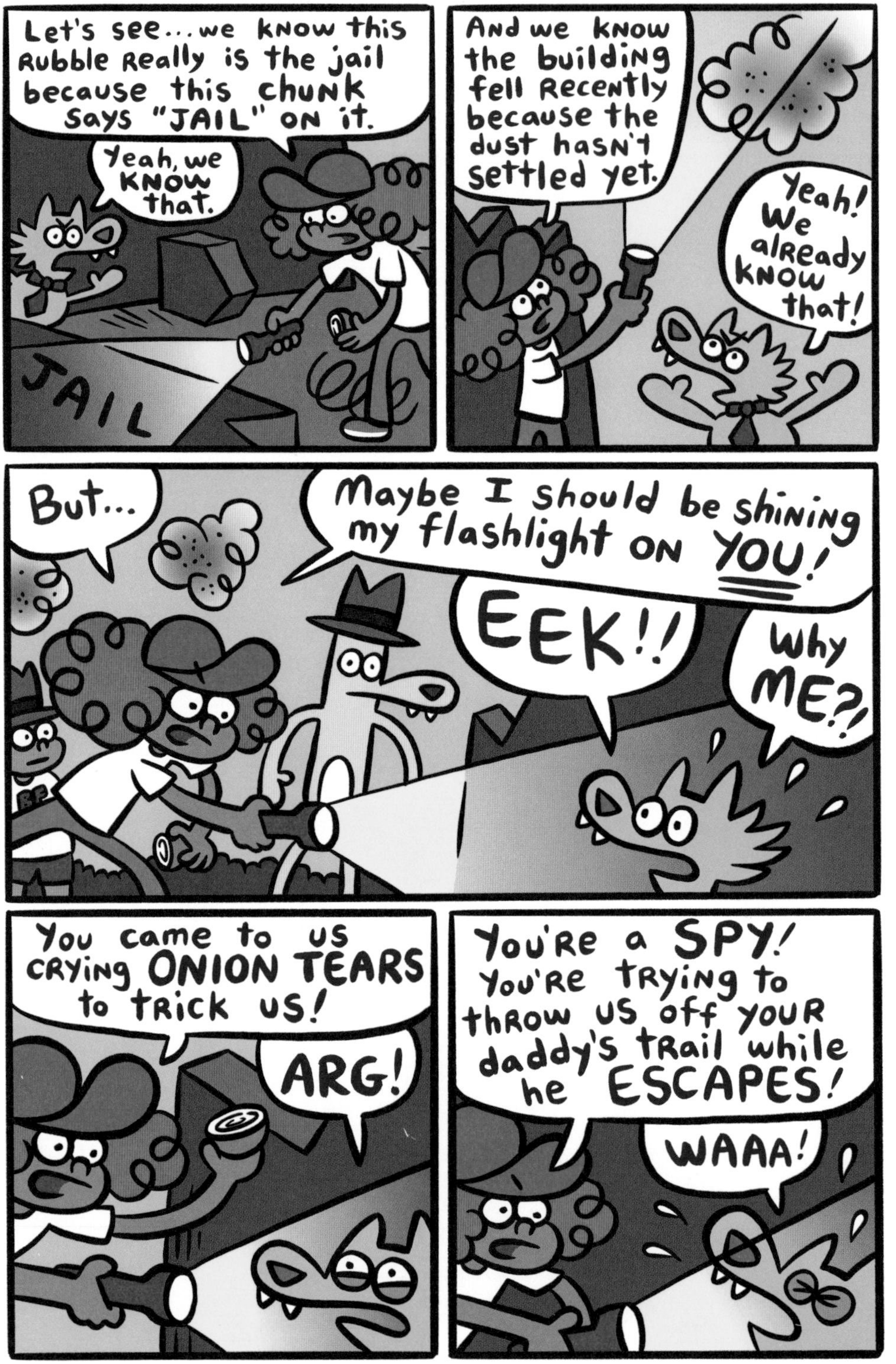

Let's see...we know this Rubble Really is the jail because this chunk says "JAIL" on it.
Yeah, we KNOW that.
JAIL
And we know the building fell Recently because the dust hasn't settled yet.
Yeah! We already KNOW that!
But...
Maybe I should be shining my flashlight on YOU!
EEK!!
Why ME?!
You came to us crying ONION TEARS to trick us!
ARG!
You're a SPY! You're trying to throw us off your daddy's trail while he ESCAPES!
WAAA!

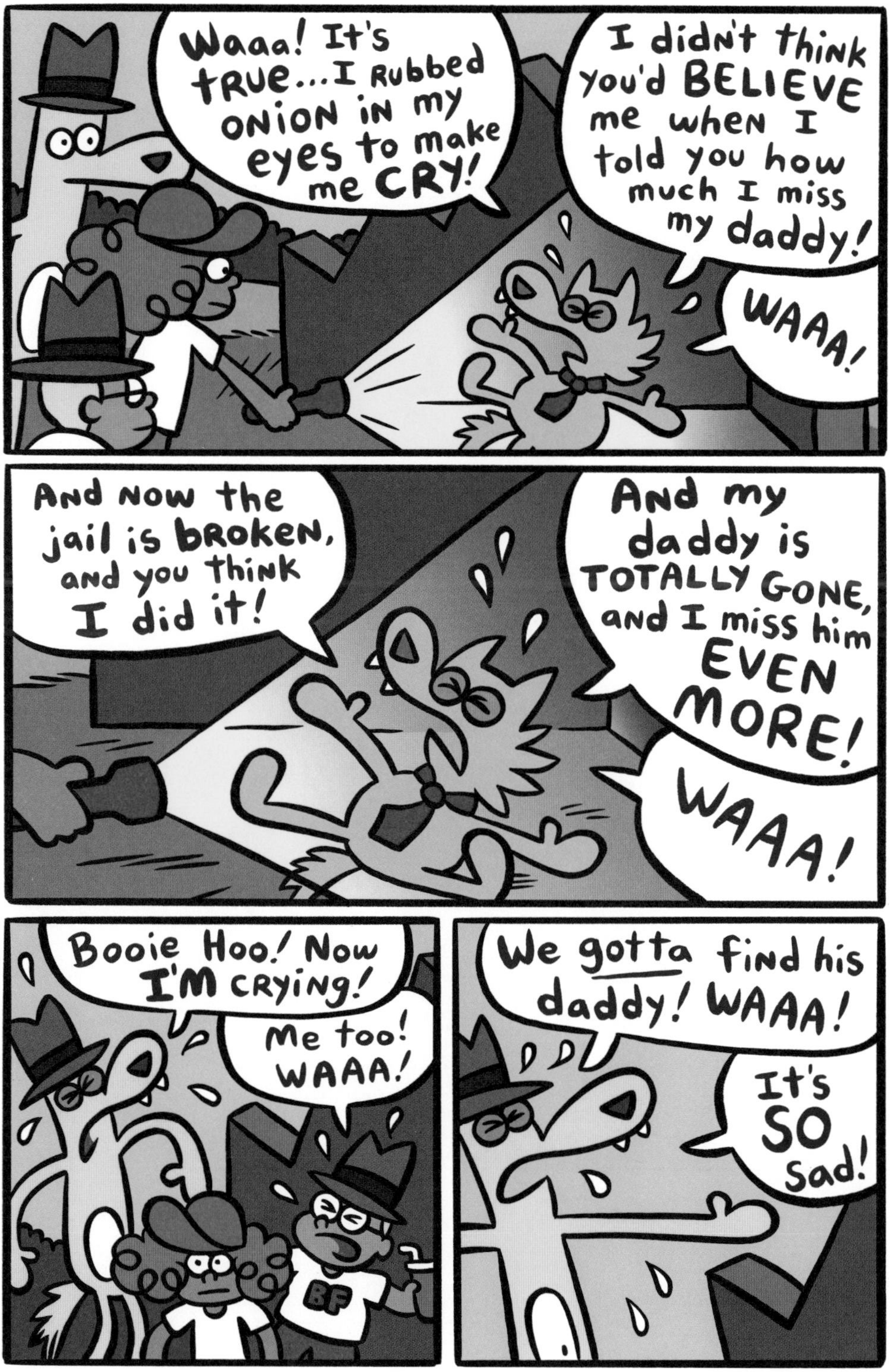
Waaa! It's TRUE...I Rubbed ONION in my eyes to make me CRY!
I didn't think you'd BELIEVE me when I told you how much I miss my daddy!
WAAA!
And now the jail is BROKEN, and you think I did it!
And my daddy is TOTALLY GONE, and I miss him EVEN MORE!
WAAA!
Booie Hoo! Now I'M CRYING!
Me too! WAAA!
BF
We gotta find his daddy! WAAA!
It's SO sad!

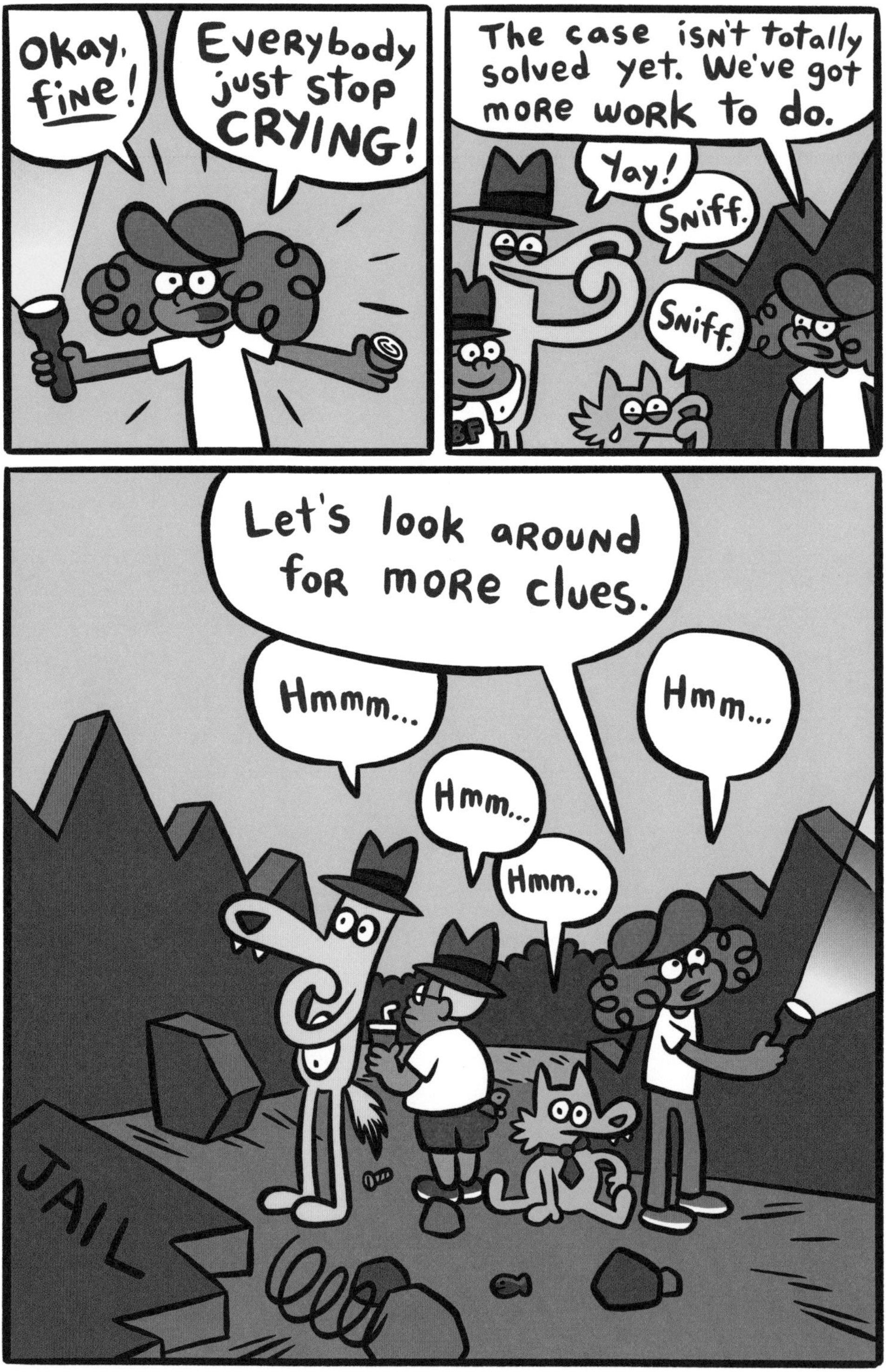
Okay, fine!
Everybody just stop CRYING!
The case isn't totally solved yet. We've got more work to do.
Yay!
Sniff.
Sniff.
BF
Let's look around for more clues.
Hmmm...
Hmm...
Hmm...
Hmm...
JAIL

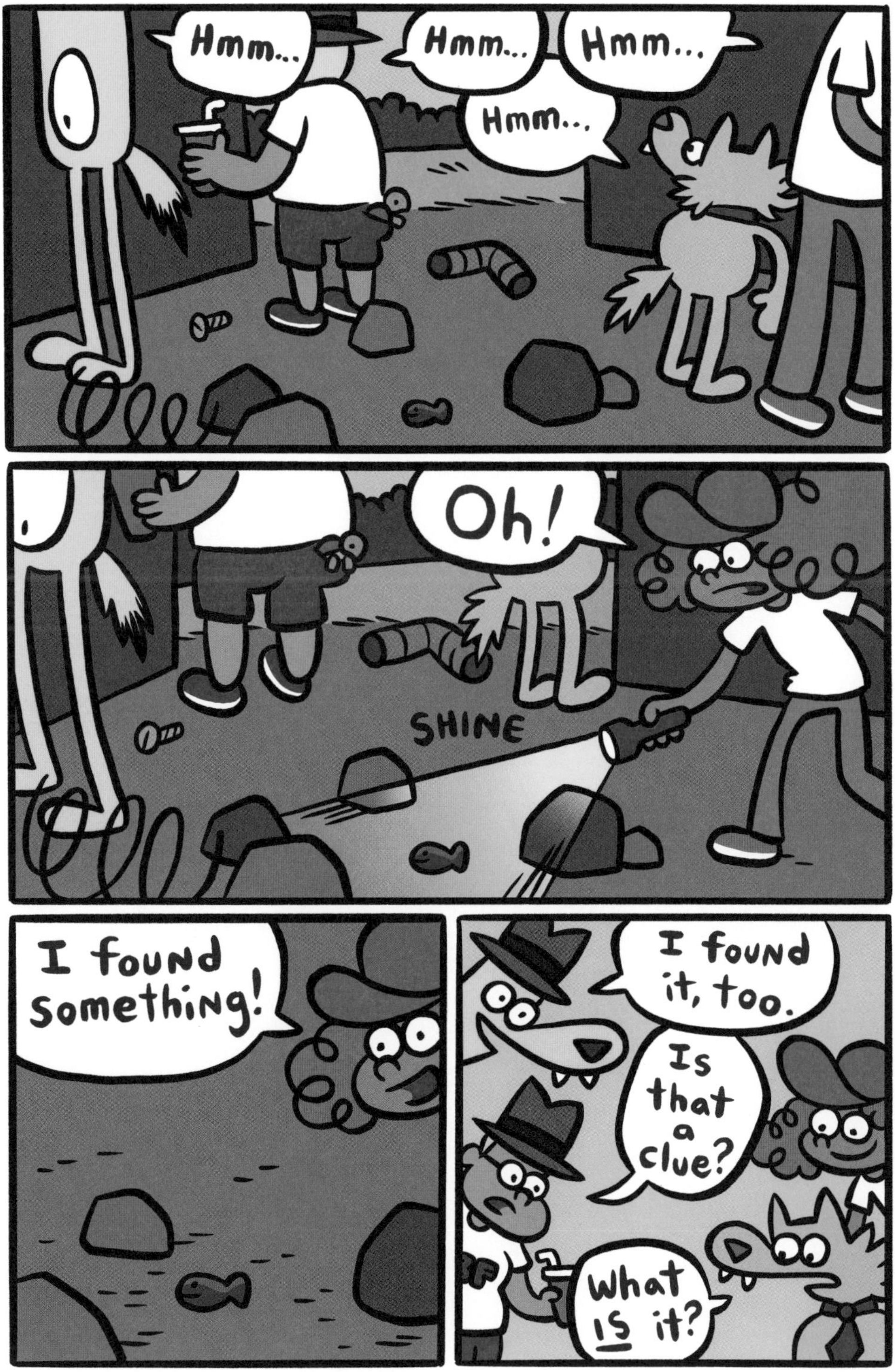
Hmm...
Hmm...
Hmm...
Hmm...
Oh!
SHINE
I found something!
I found it, too.
Is that a clue?
What IS it?

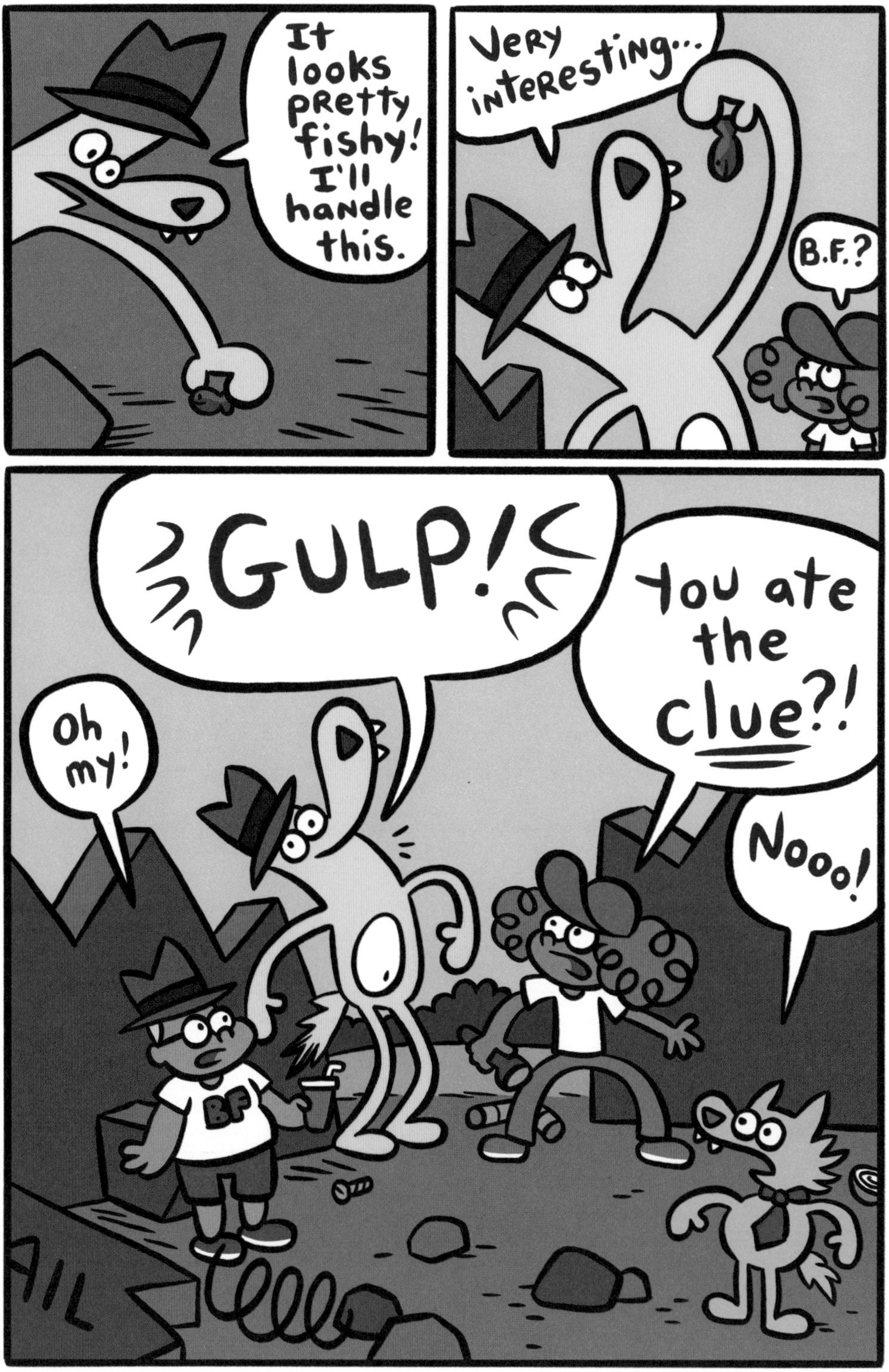
It looks pretty fishy! I'll handle this.
Very interesting...
B.F.?
GULP!
You ate the clue?!
Oh my!
Nooo!

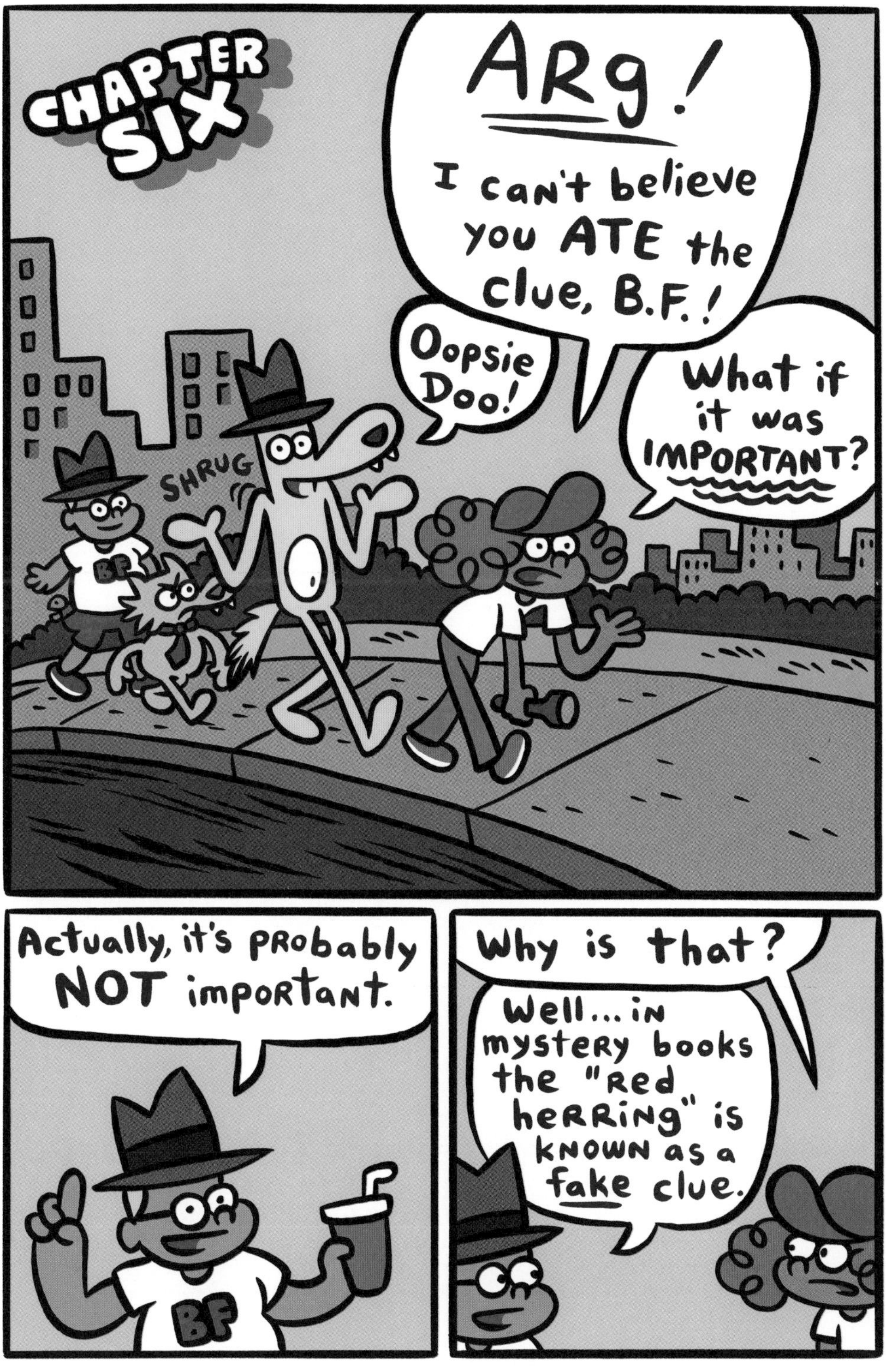
CHAPTER SIX
ARg!
I can't believe you ATE the clue, B.F.!
Oopsie Doo!
SHRUG
What if it was IMPORTANT?
Actually, it's probably NOT important.
Why is that?
Well... in mystery books the "red herring" is known as a fake clue.

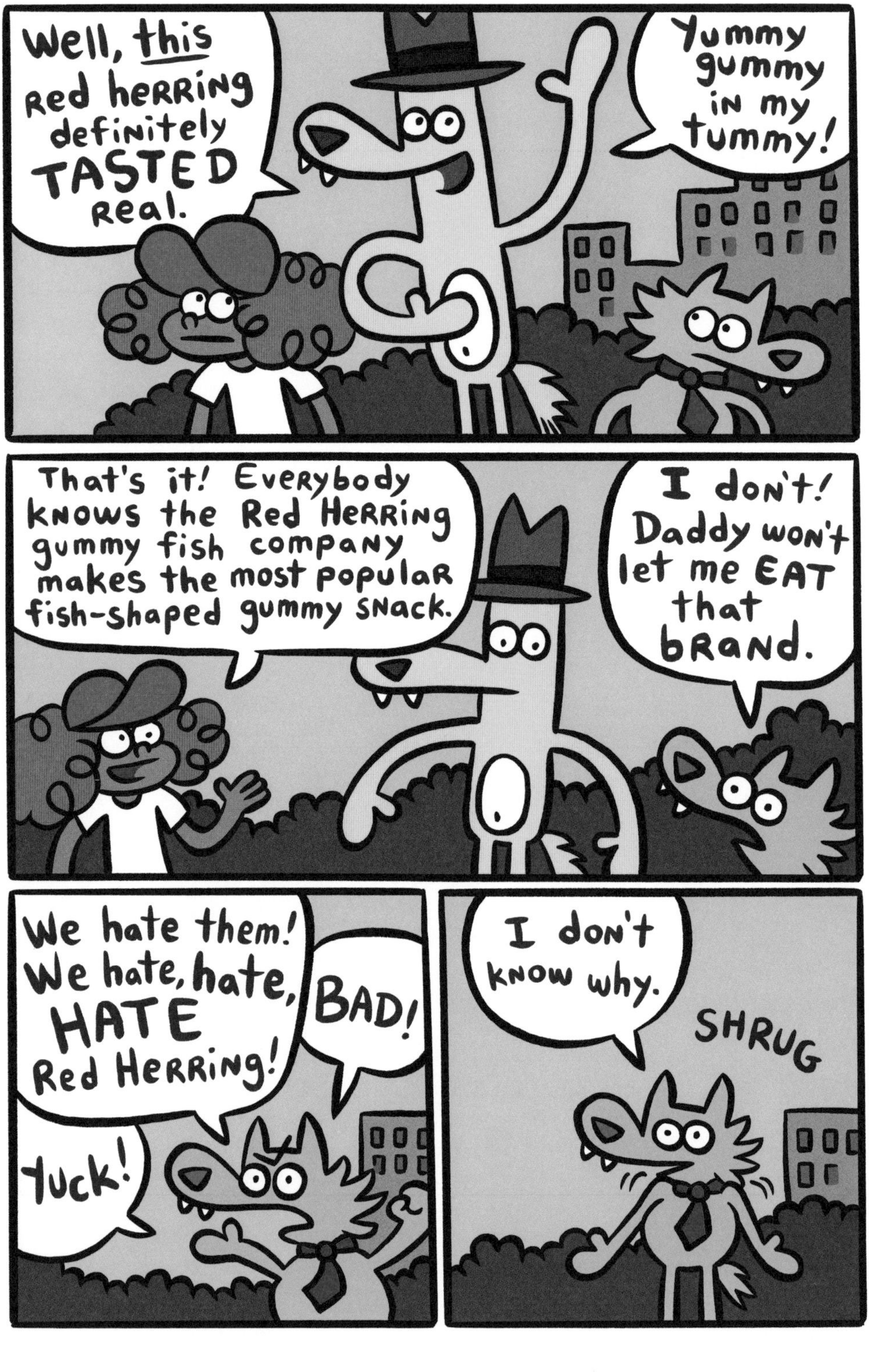
Well, this red herring definitely TASTED real.
Yummy gummy in my tummy!
That's it! Everybody knows the Red Herring gummy fish company makes the most popular fish-shaped gummy snack.
I don't! Daddy won't let me EAT that brand.
We hate them! We hate, hate, HATE Red Herring!
BAD!
Yuck!
I don't know why.
SHRUG

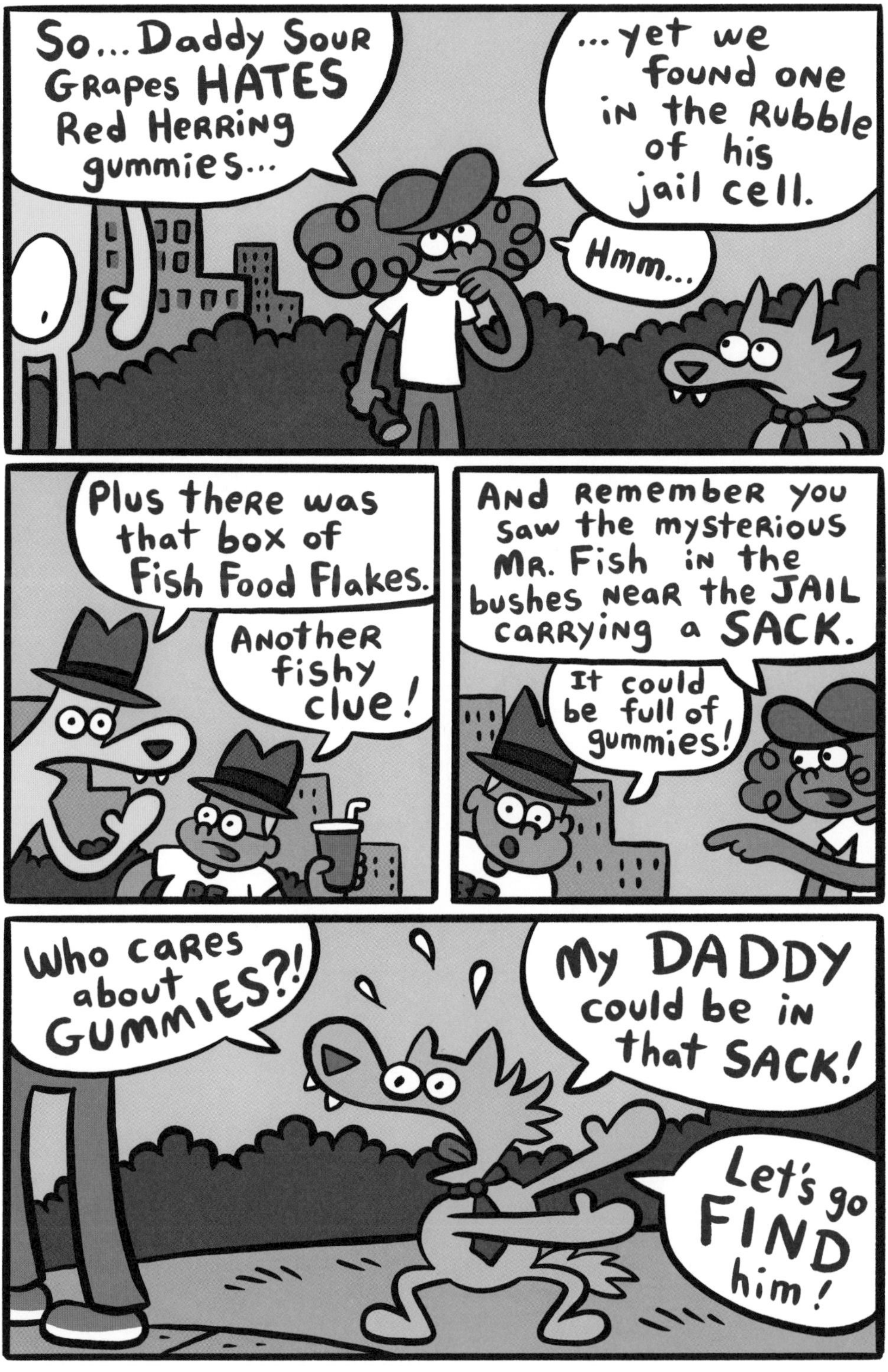
So... Daddy Sour Grapes HATES Red Herring gummies...
...yet we found one in the rubble of his jail cell.
Hmm...
Plus there was that box of Fish Food Flakes.
Another fishy clue!
And remember you saw the mysterious Mr. Fish in the bushes near the JAIL carrying a SACK.
It could be full of gummies!
Who cares about GUMMIES?!
My DADDY could be in that SACK!
Let's go FIND him!

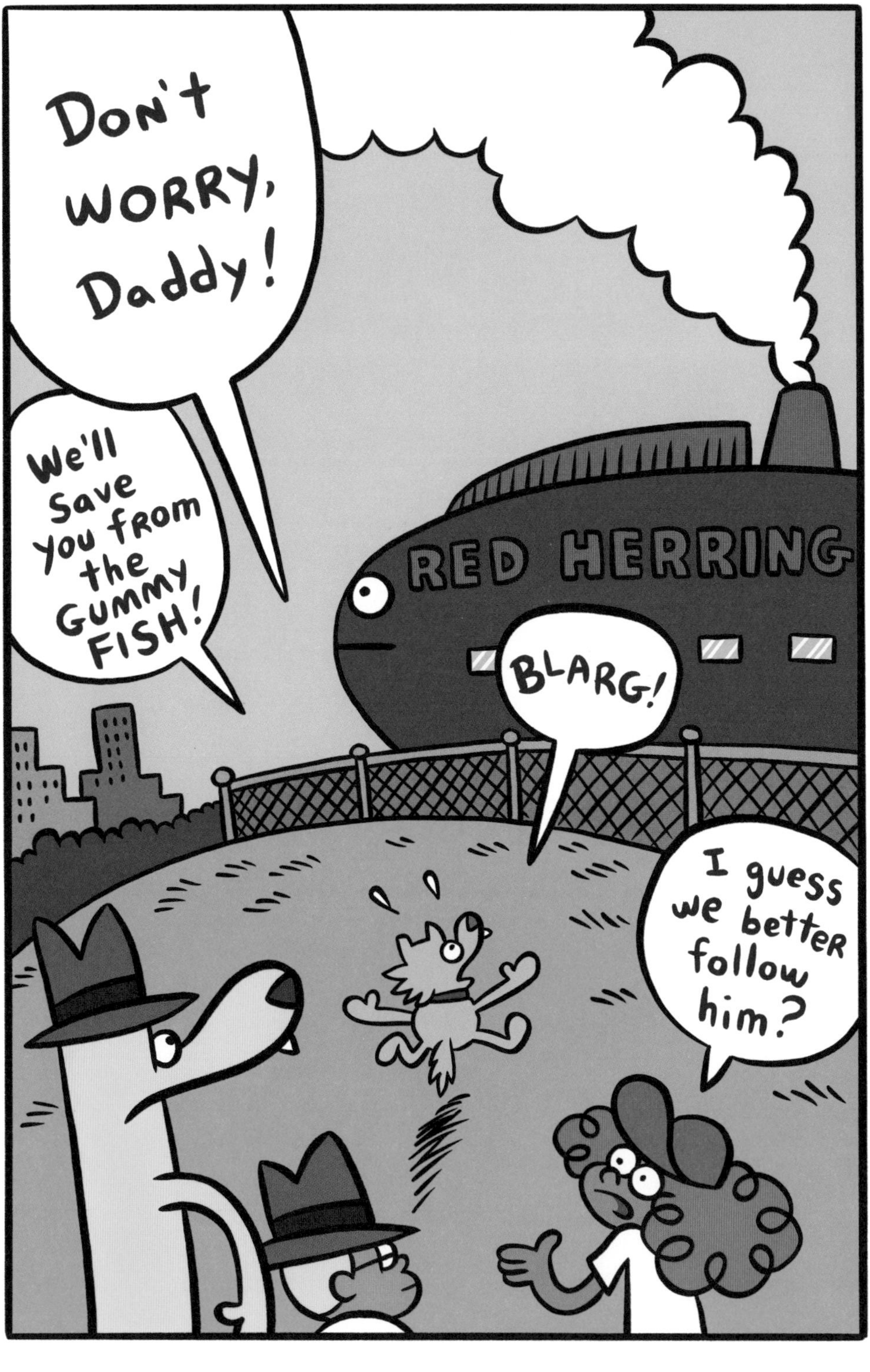
RED HERRING
Don't WORRY, Daddy!
We'll save you from the GUMMY FISH!
BLARG!
I guess we better follow him?

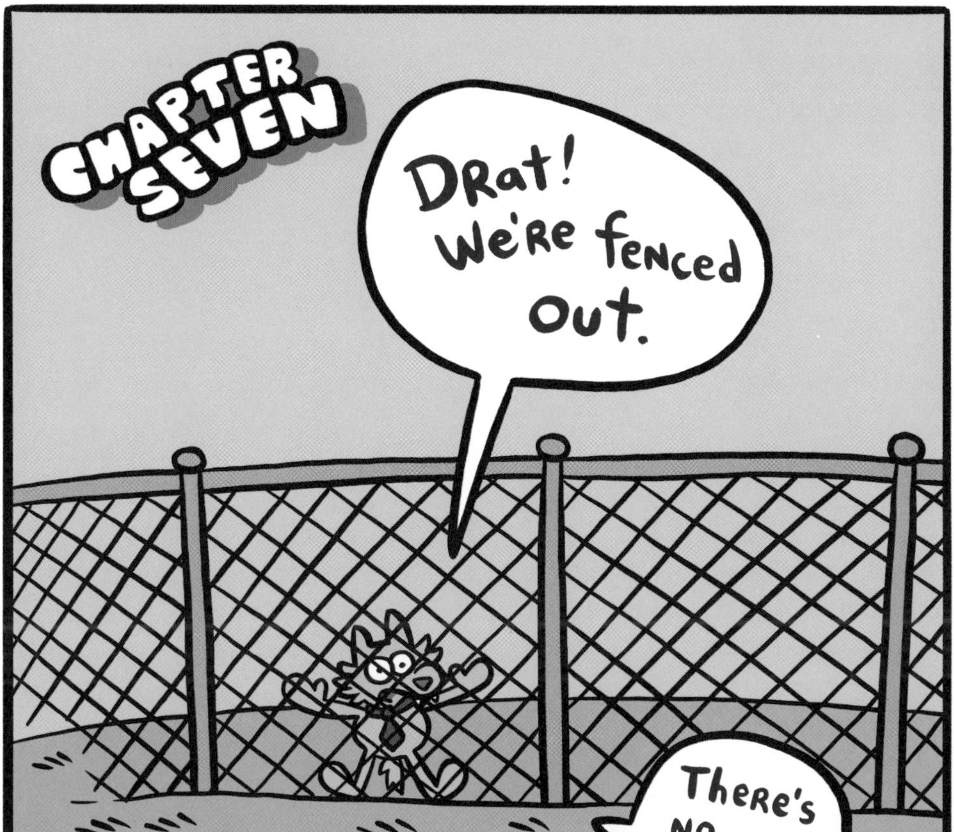
CHAPTER SEVEN
DRat! We're fenced out.
There's no way in.

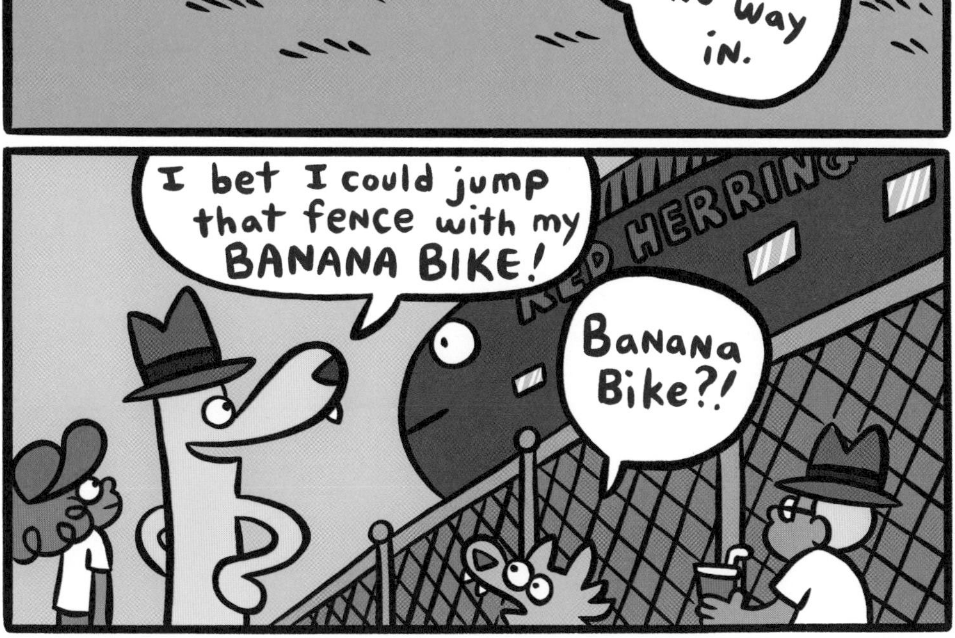
I bet I could jump that fence with my BANANA BIKE!
RED HERRING
Banana Bike?!

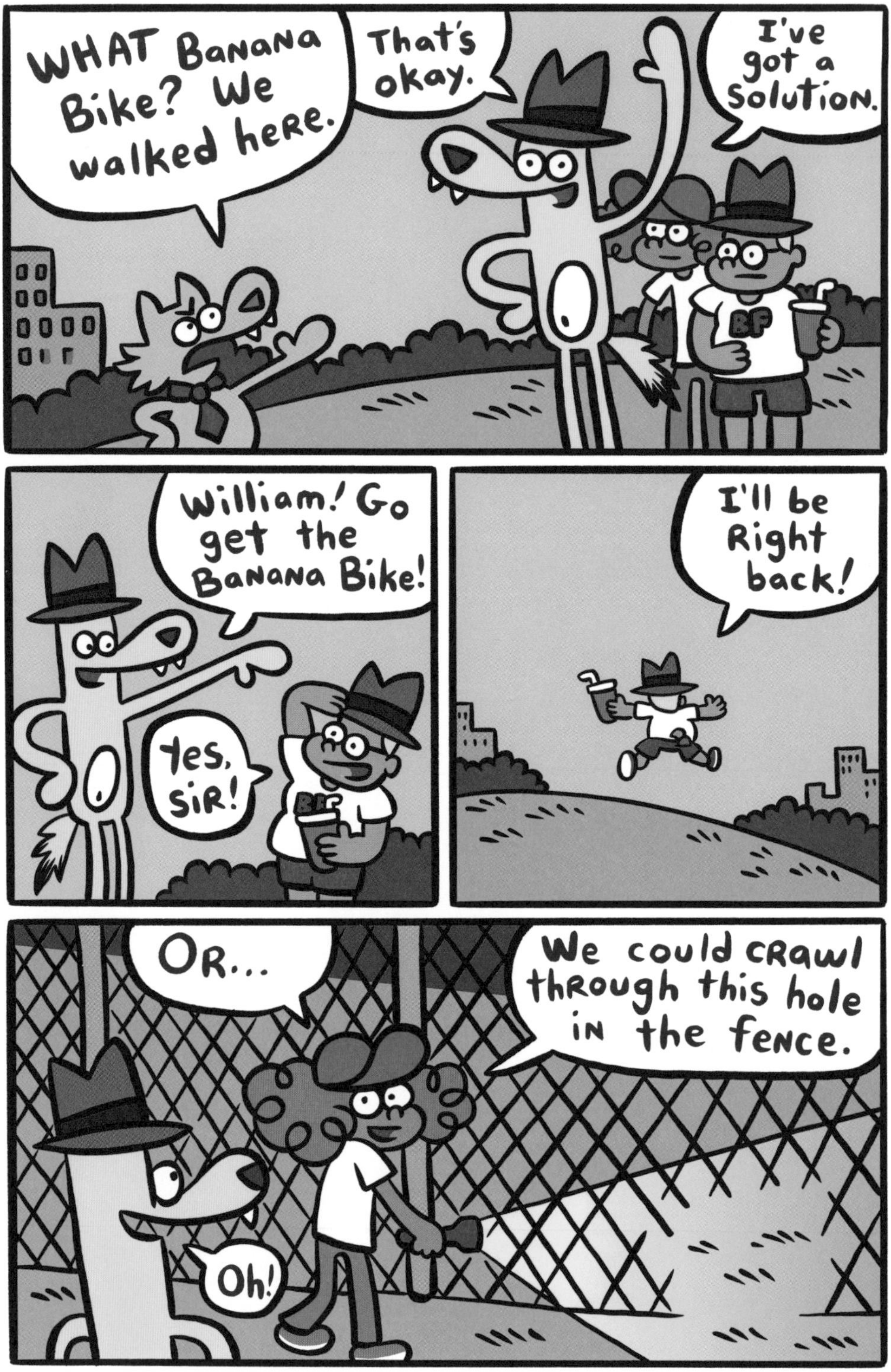
WHAT Banana Bike? We walked here.
That's okay.
I've got a solution.
William! Go get the Banana Bike!
Yes, sir!
I'll be right back!
Or...
We could crawl through this hole in the fence.
Oh!

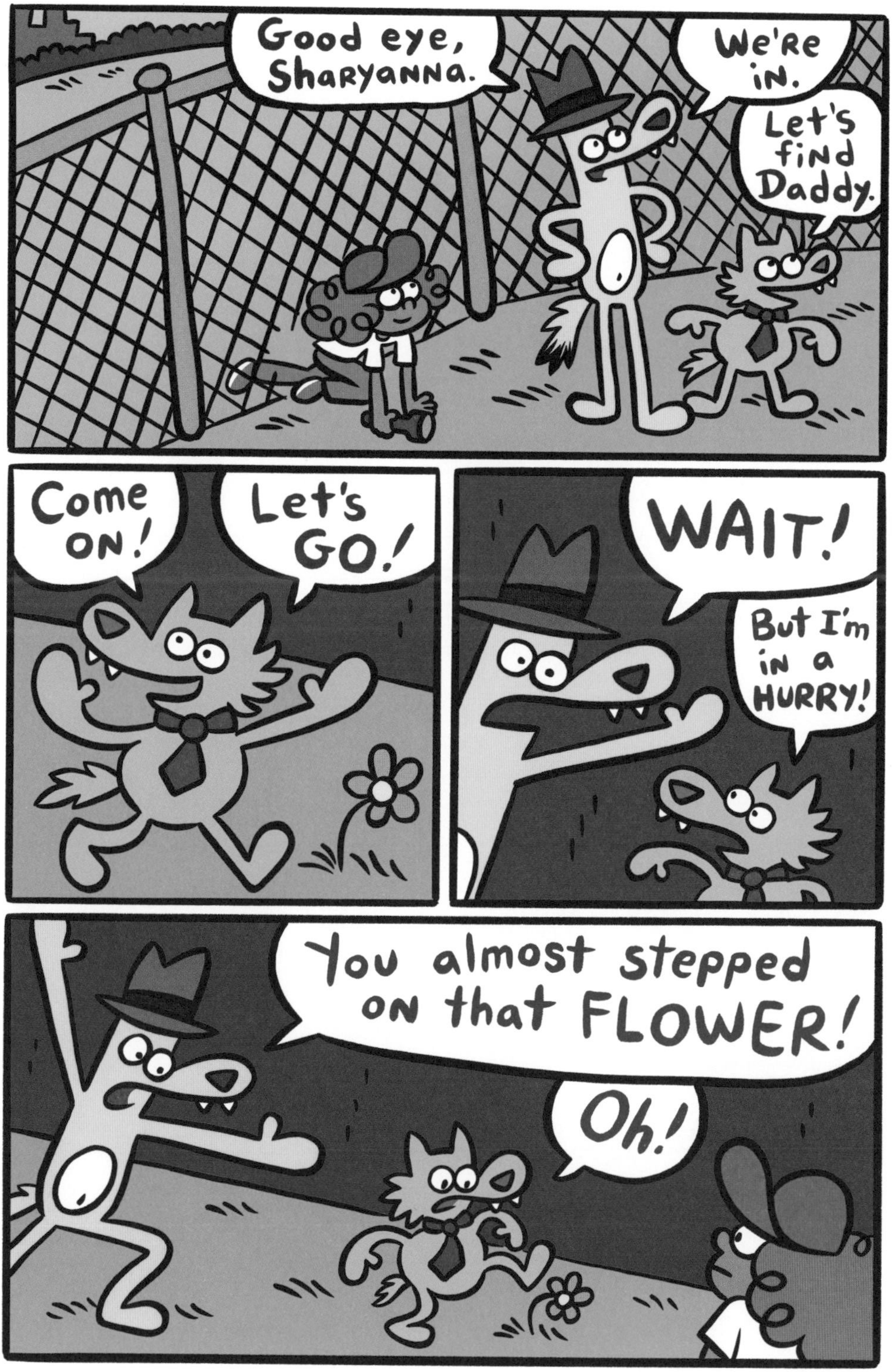
Good eye, Sharyanna.
We're in.
Let's find Daddy.
Come on!
Let's GO!
WAIT!
But I'm in a HURRY!
You almost stepped on that FLOWER!
Oh!

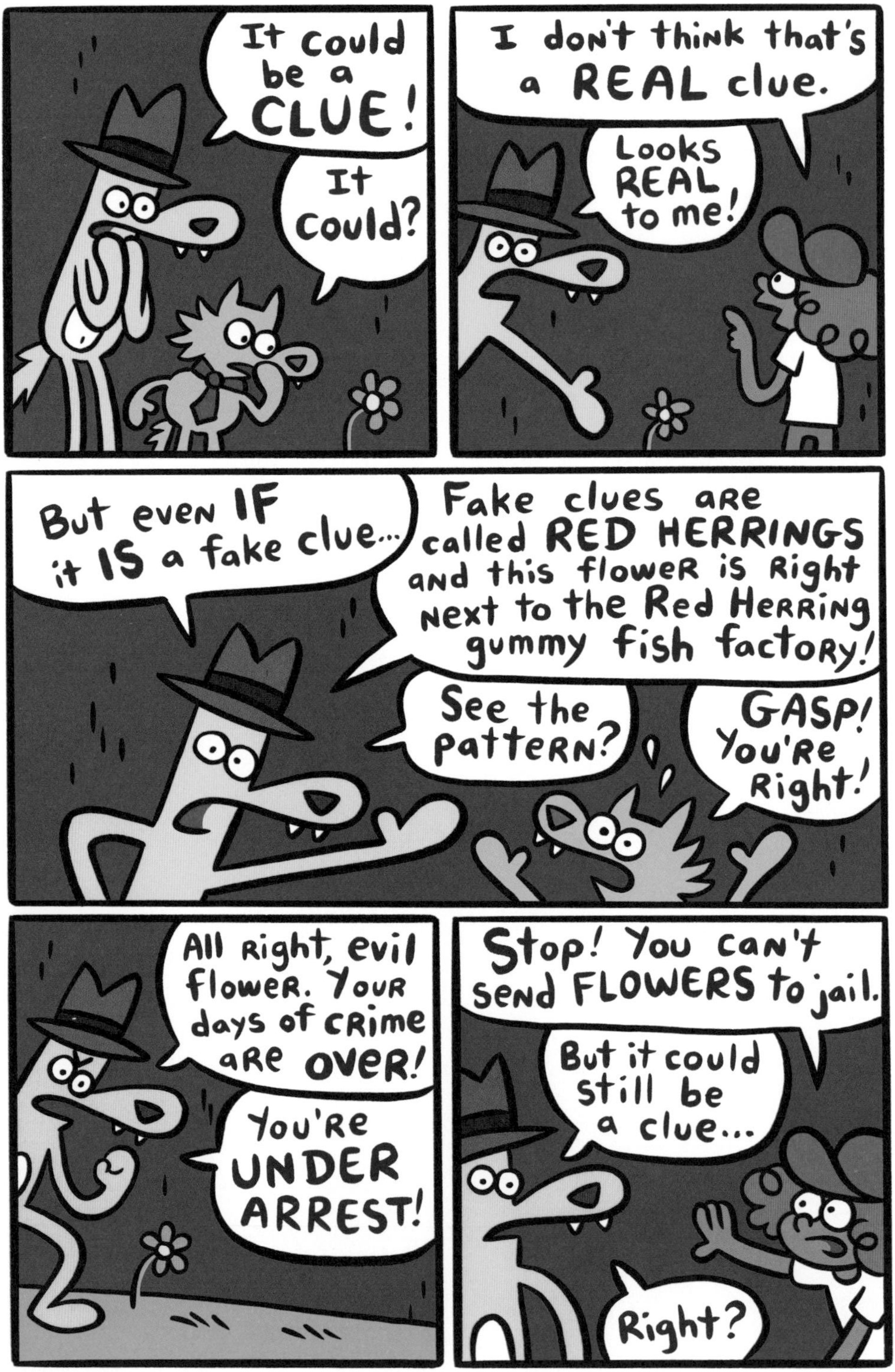
It could be a CLUE!
It could?
I don't think that's a REAL clue.
Looks REAL to me!
But even IF it IS a fake clue...
Fake clues are called RED HERRINGS and this flower is Right next to the Red Herring gummy fish factory!
See the pattern?
GASP! You're Right!
All Right, evil flower. Your days of crime are OVER!
You're UNDER ARREST!
Stop! You can't send FLOWERS to jail.
But it could still be a clue...
Right?

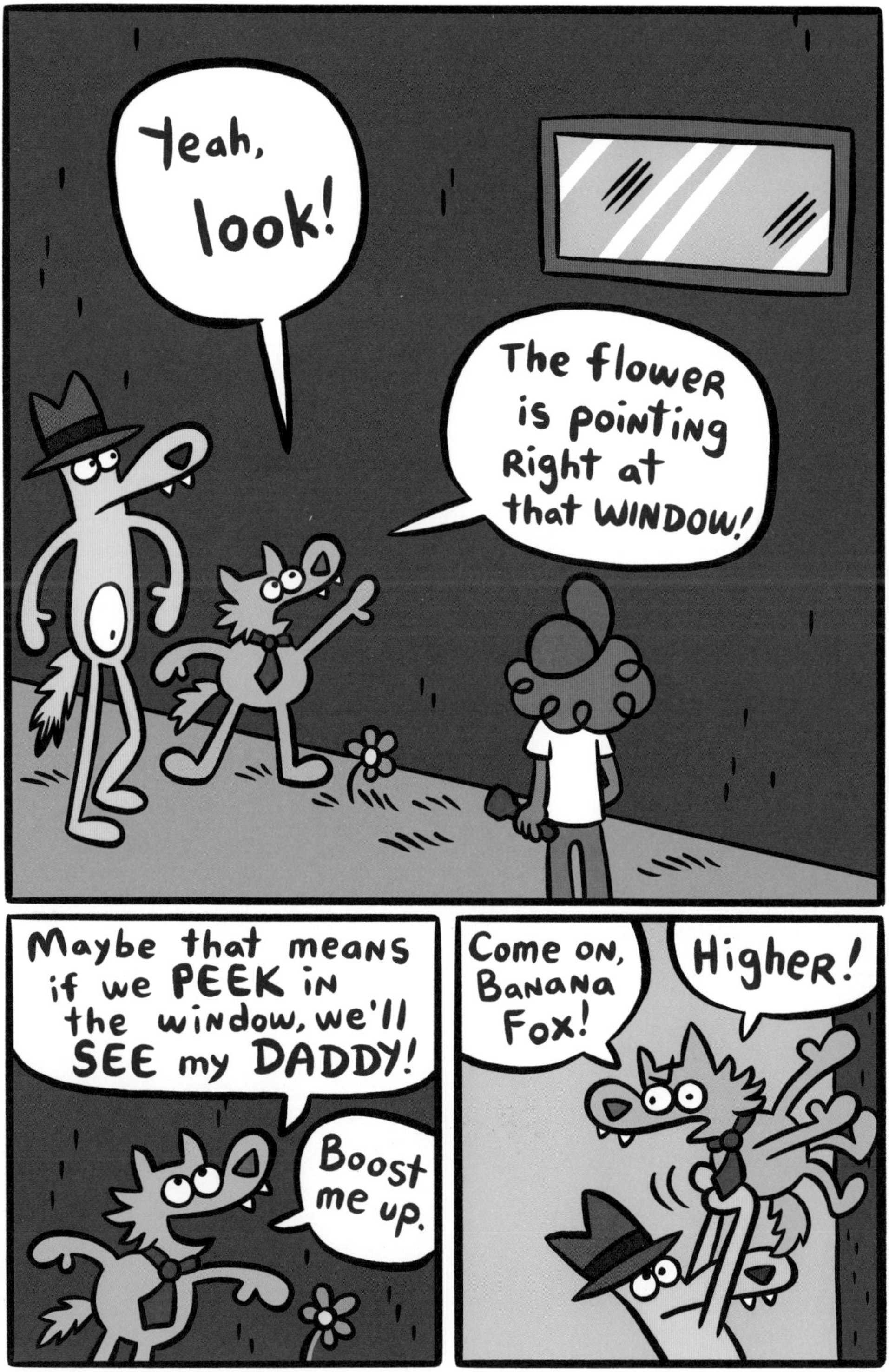
Yeah, look!
The flower is pointing Right at that WINDOW!
Maybe that means if we PEEK in the window, we'll SEE my DADDY!
Boost me up.
Come on, Banana Fox!
Higher!

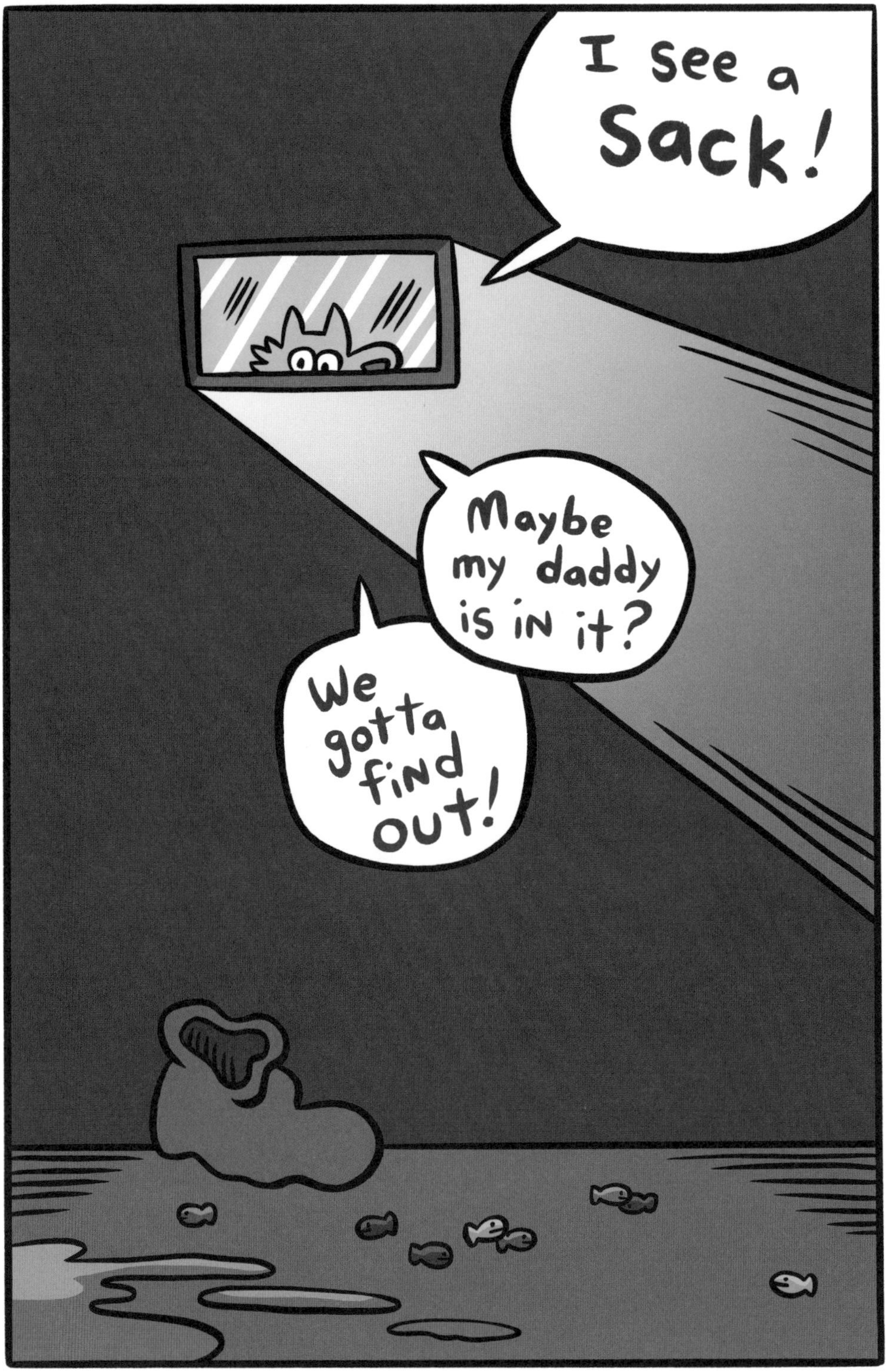
I see a Sack!
Maybe my daddy is in it?
We gotta find out!

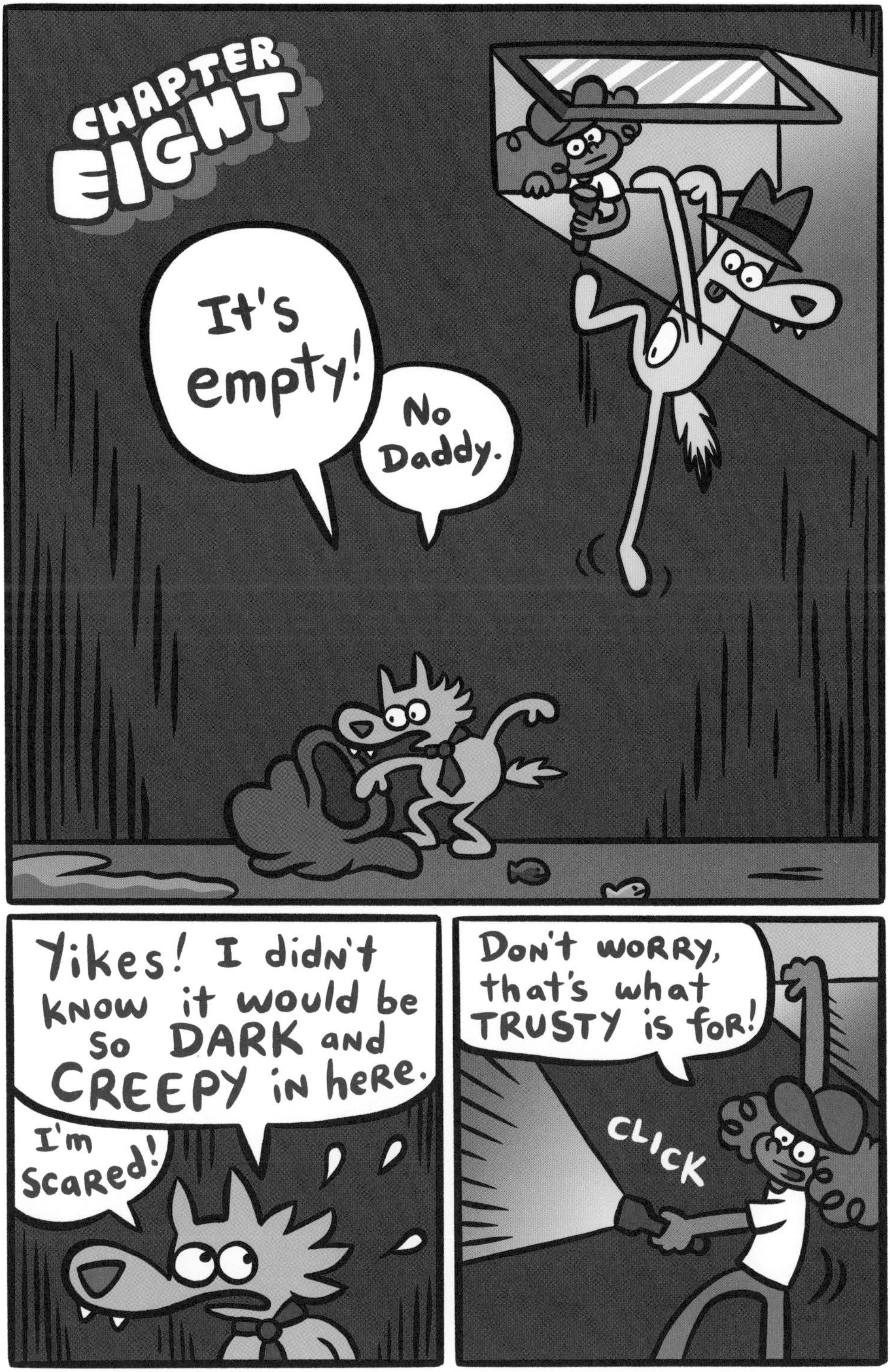
CHAPTER EIGHT
It's empty!
No Daddy.
Yikes! I didn't know it would be so DARK and CREEPY in here.
I'm scared!
Don't worry, that's what TRUSTY is for!
CLICK

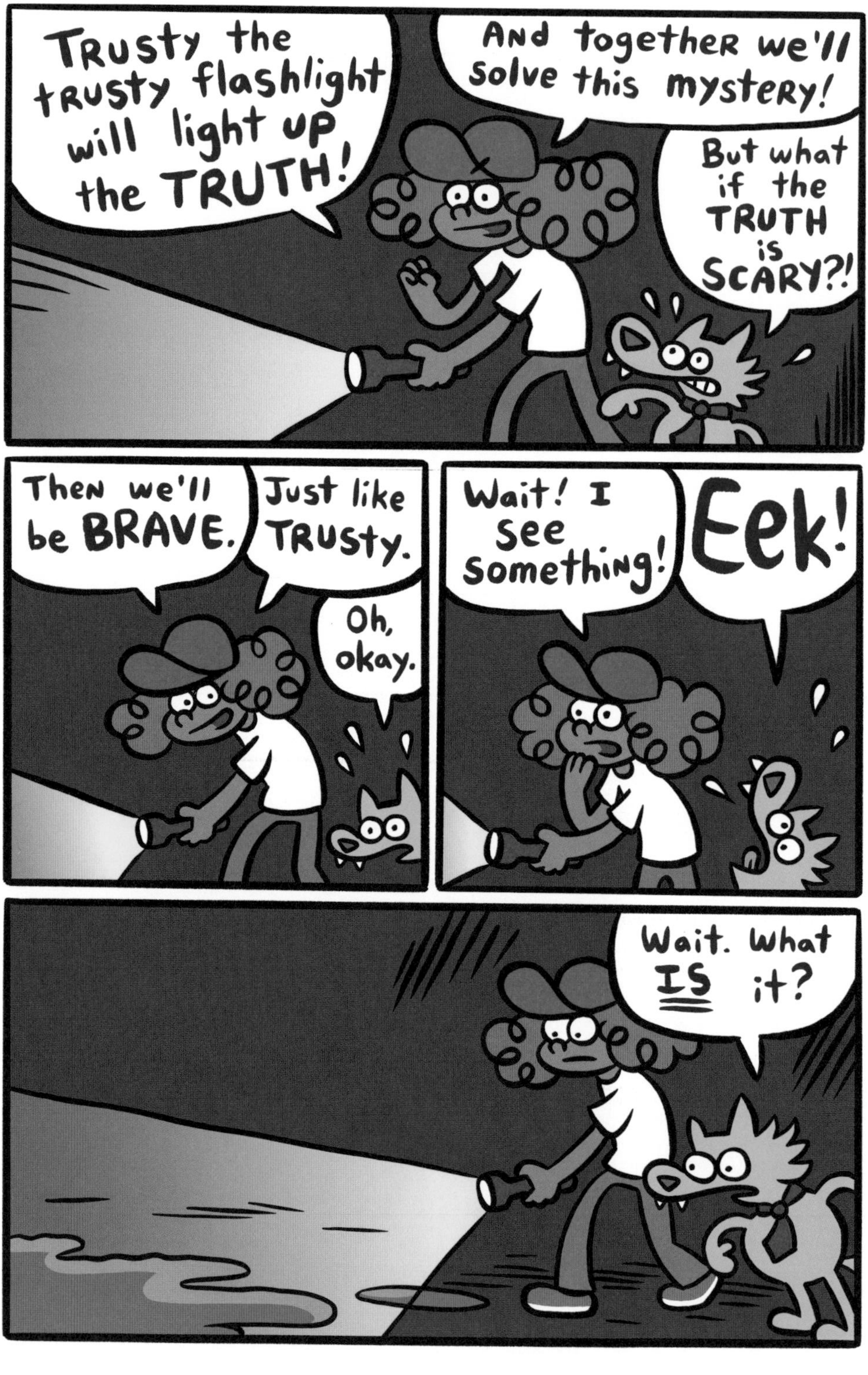
Trusty the trusty flashlight will light up the TRUTH!
And together we'll solve this mystery!
But what if the TRUTH is SCARY?!
Then we'll be BRAVE.
Just like TRUSTY.
Oh, okay.
Wait! I see something!
Eek!
Wait. What IS it?

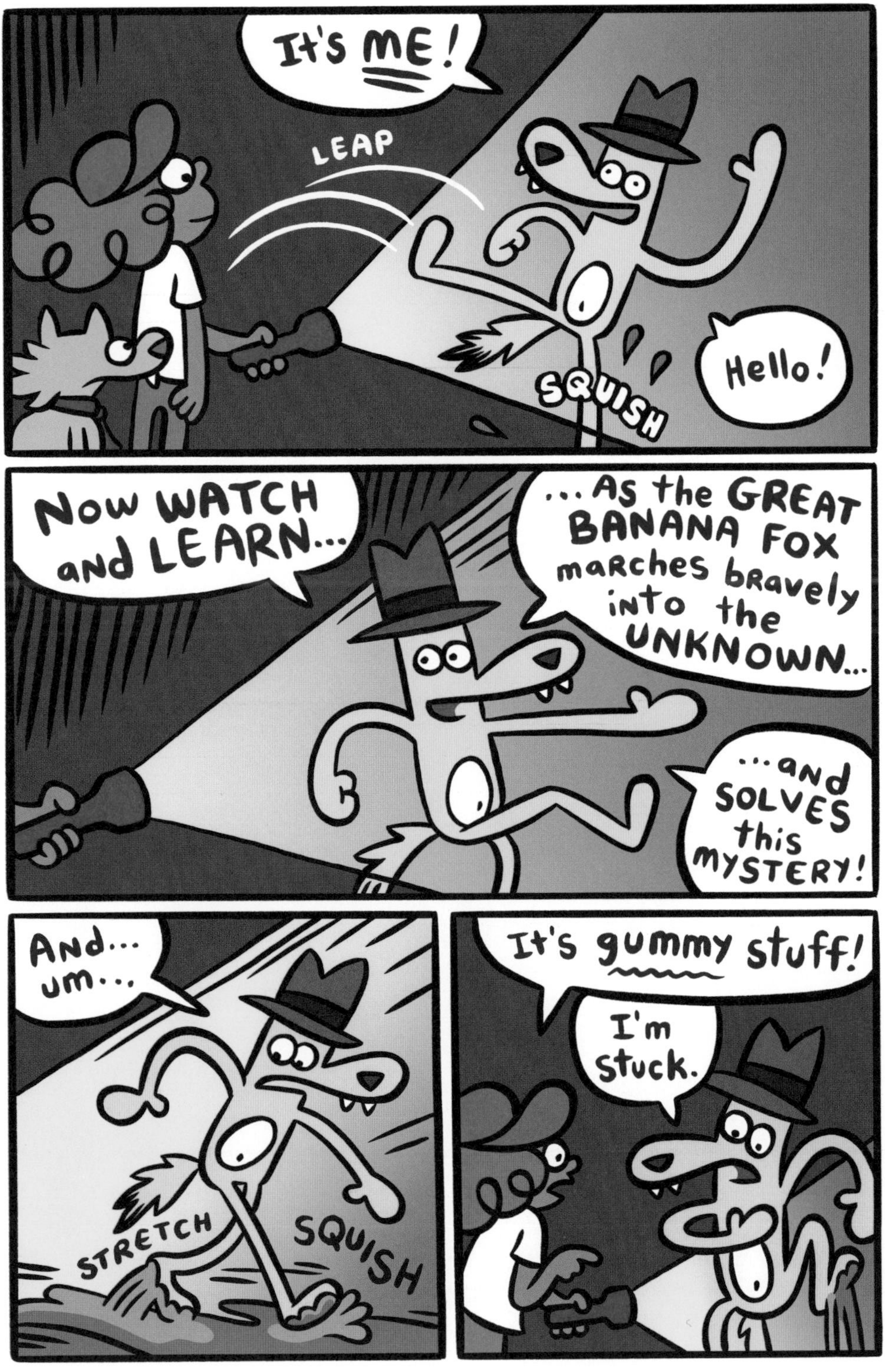
It's ME!
LEAP
Hello!
SQUISH
Now WATCH and LEARN...
...As the GREAT BANANA FOX marches bravely into the UNKNOWN...
...and SOLVES this MYSTERY!
And... um...
STRETCH
SQUISH
It's gummy stuff!
I'm stuck.

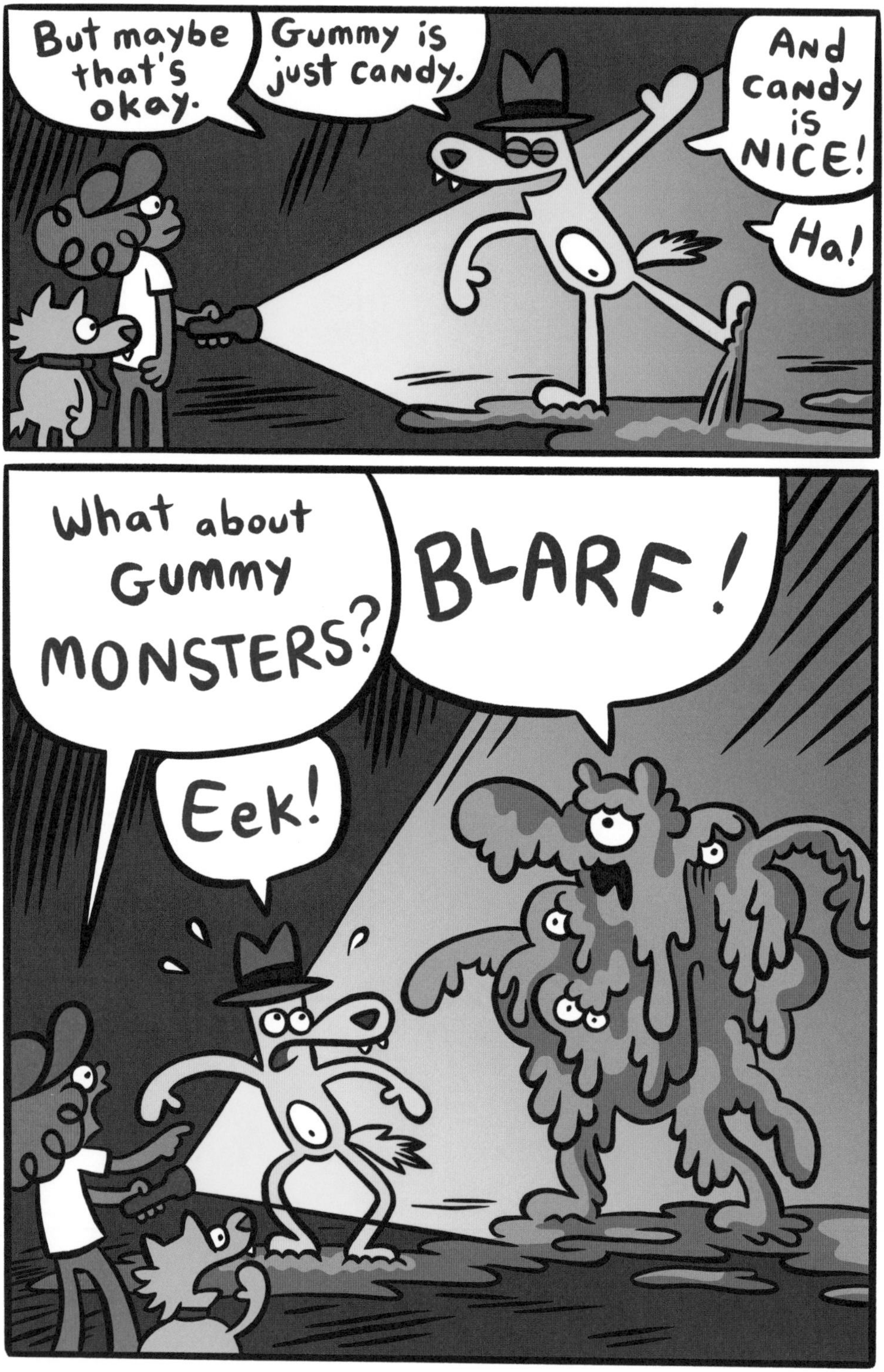
But maybe that's okay.
Gummy is just candy.
And candy is NICE!
Ha!
What about GUMMY MONSTERS?
BLARF!
Eek!

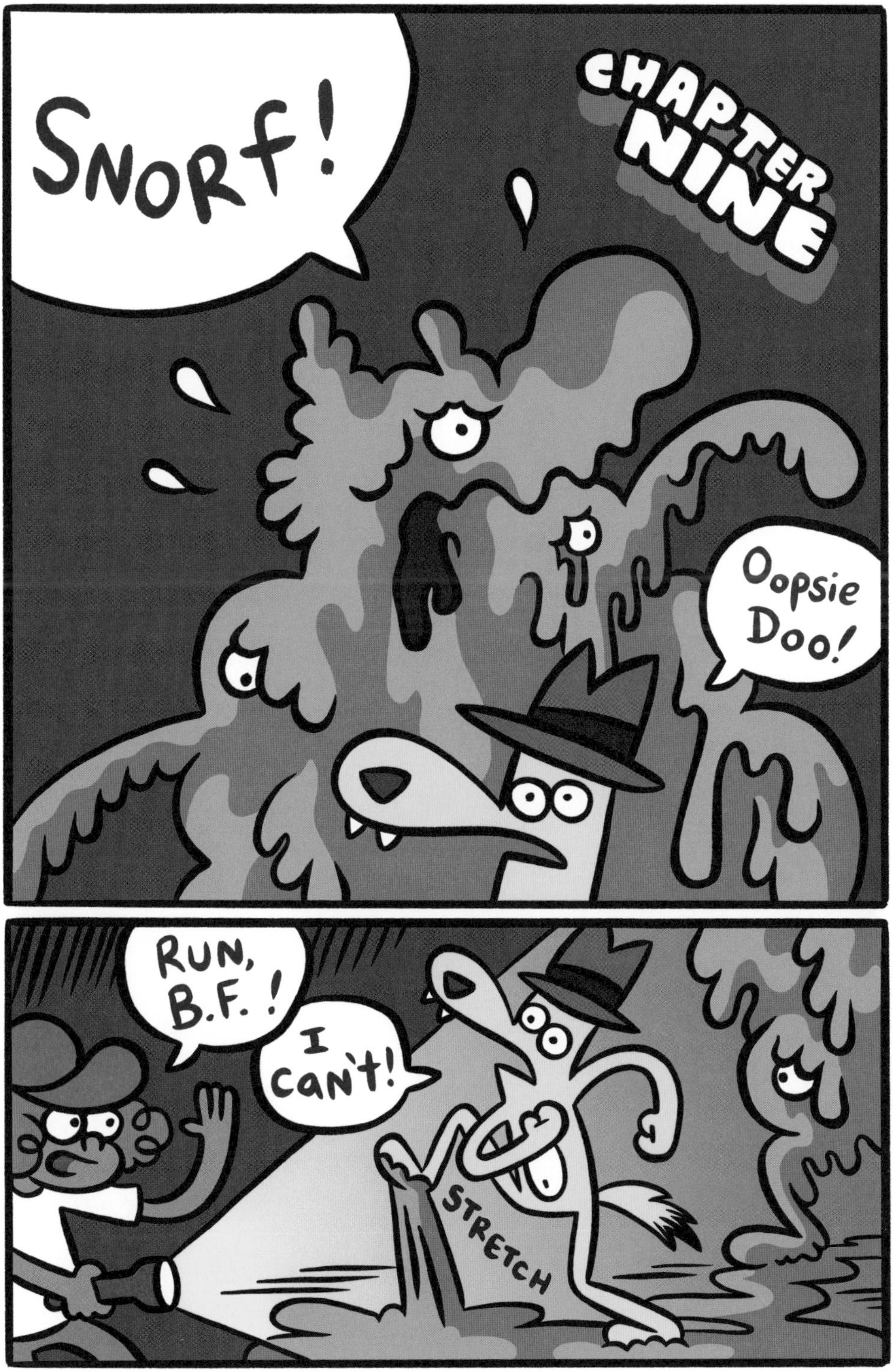
SNORF!
CHAPTER NINE
Oopsie Doo!
RUN, B.F.!
I can't!
STRETCH

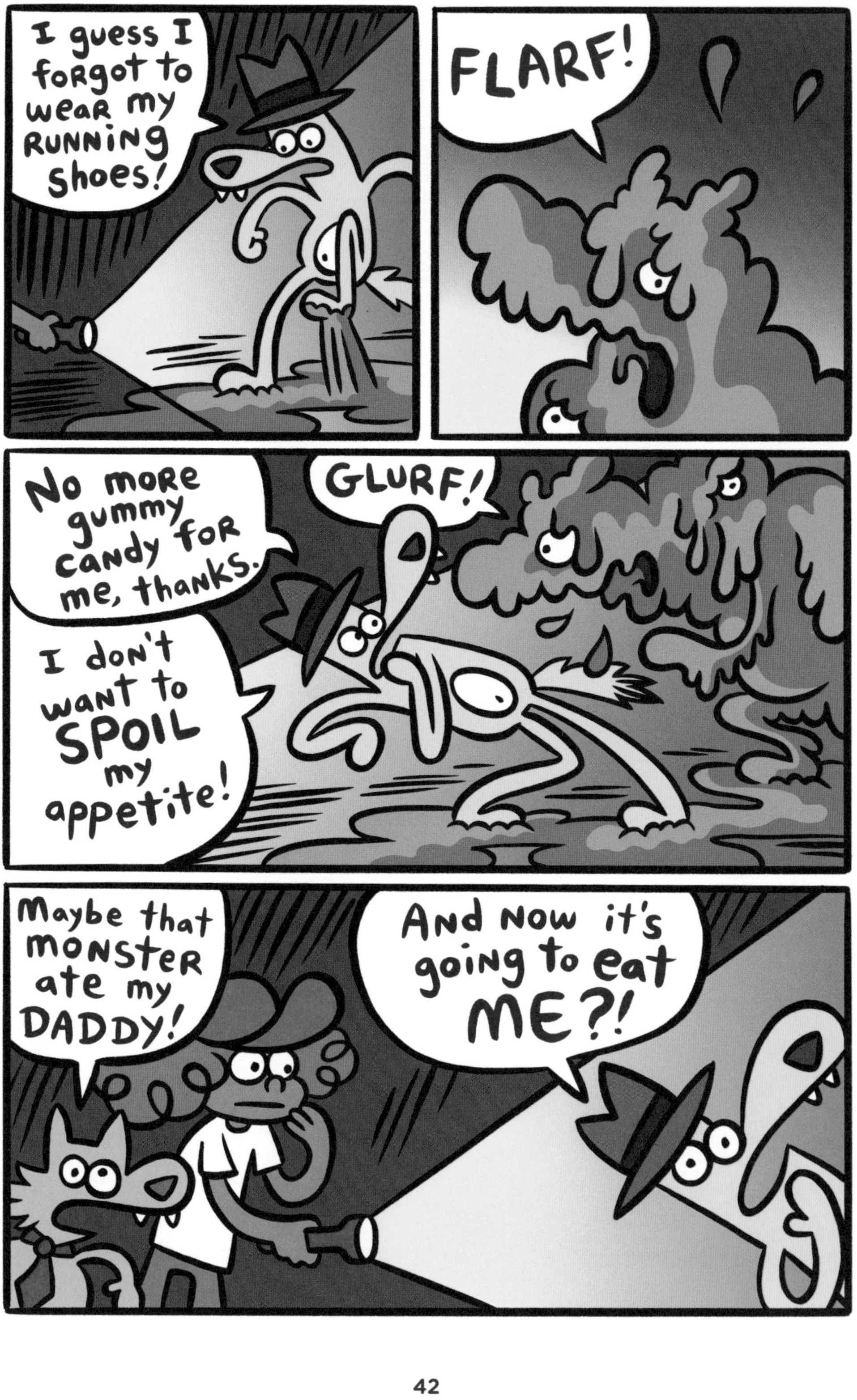
I guess I forgot to wear my RUNNING shoes!
FLARF!
No more gummy candy for me, thanks.
GLURF!
I don't want to SPOIL my appetite!
Maybe that MONSTER ate my DADDY!
And now it's going to eat ME?!

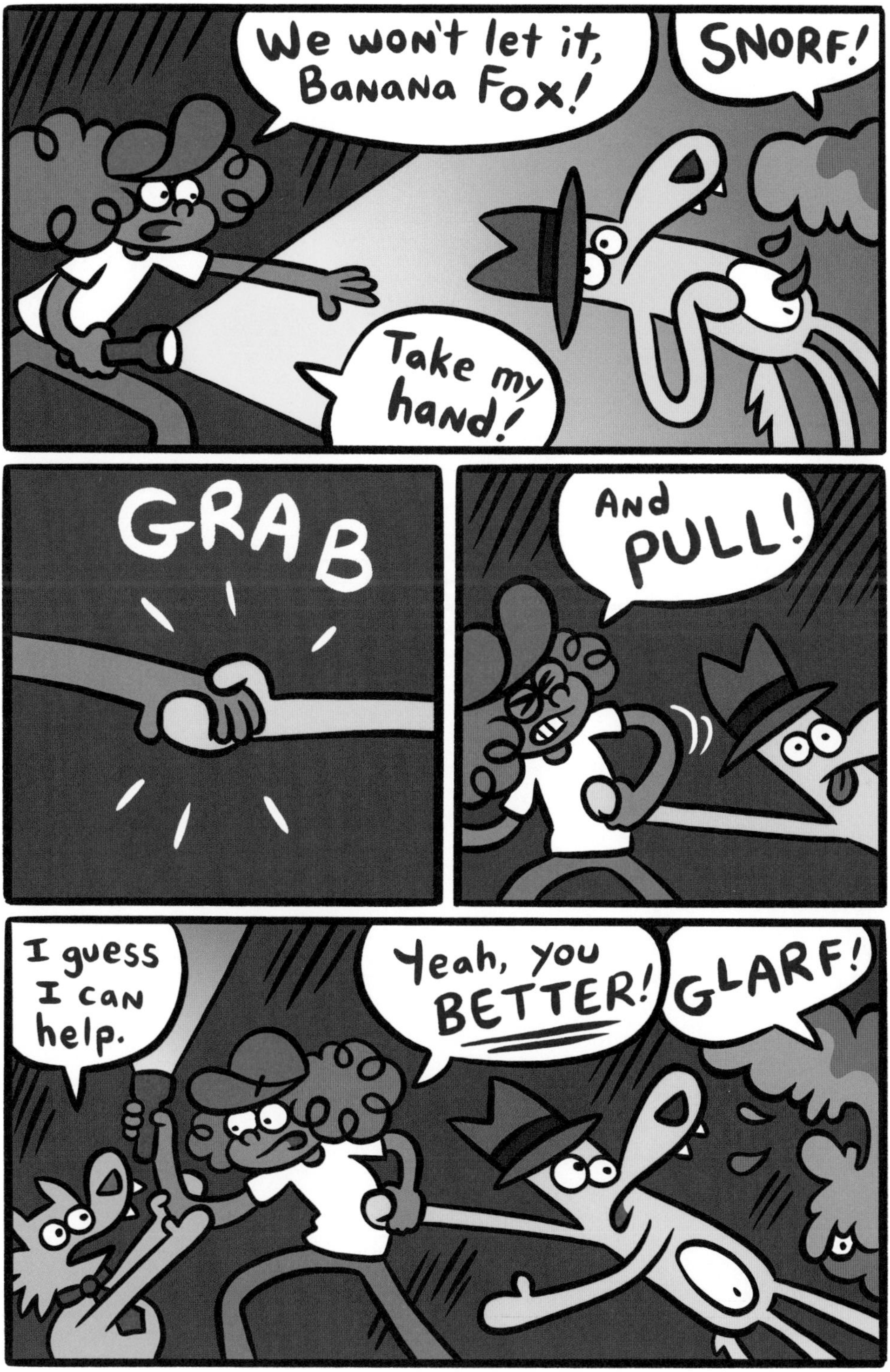
We won't let it, Banana Fox!
SNORF!
Take my hand!
GRAB
AND PULL!
I guess I can help.
Yeah, you BETTER!
GLARF!

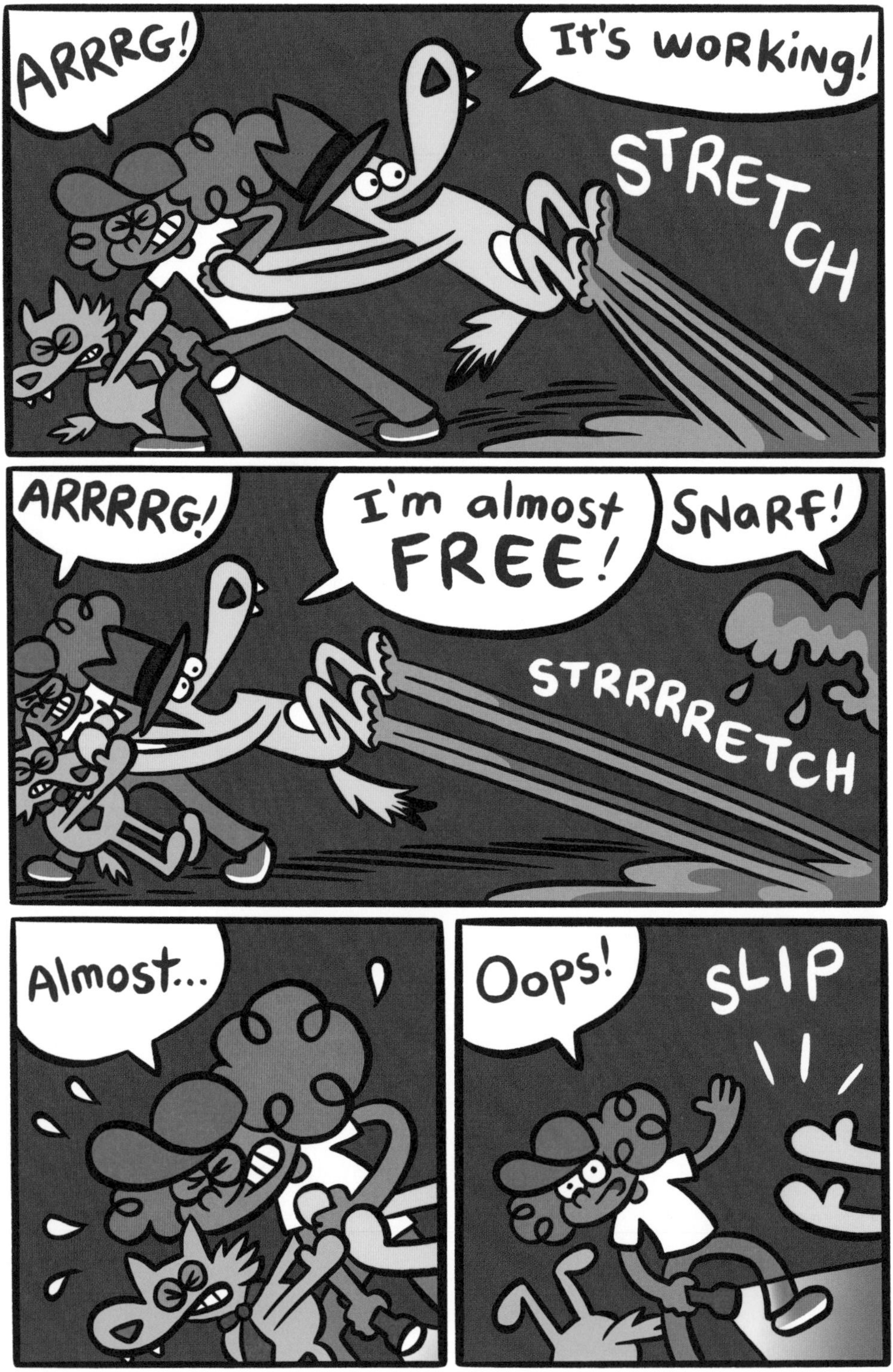
ARRRG!
It's working!
STRETCH
ARRRRG!
I'm almost FREE!
SNARF!
STRRRRRETCH
Almost...
Oops!
SLIP

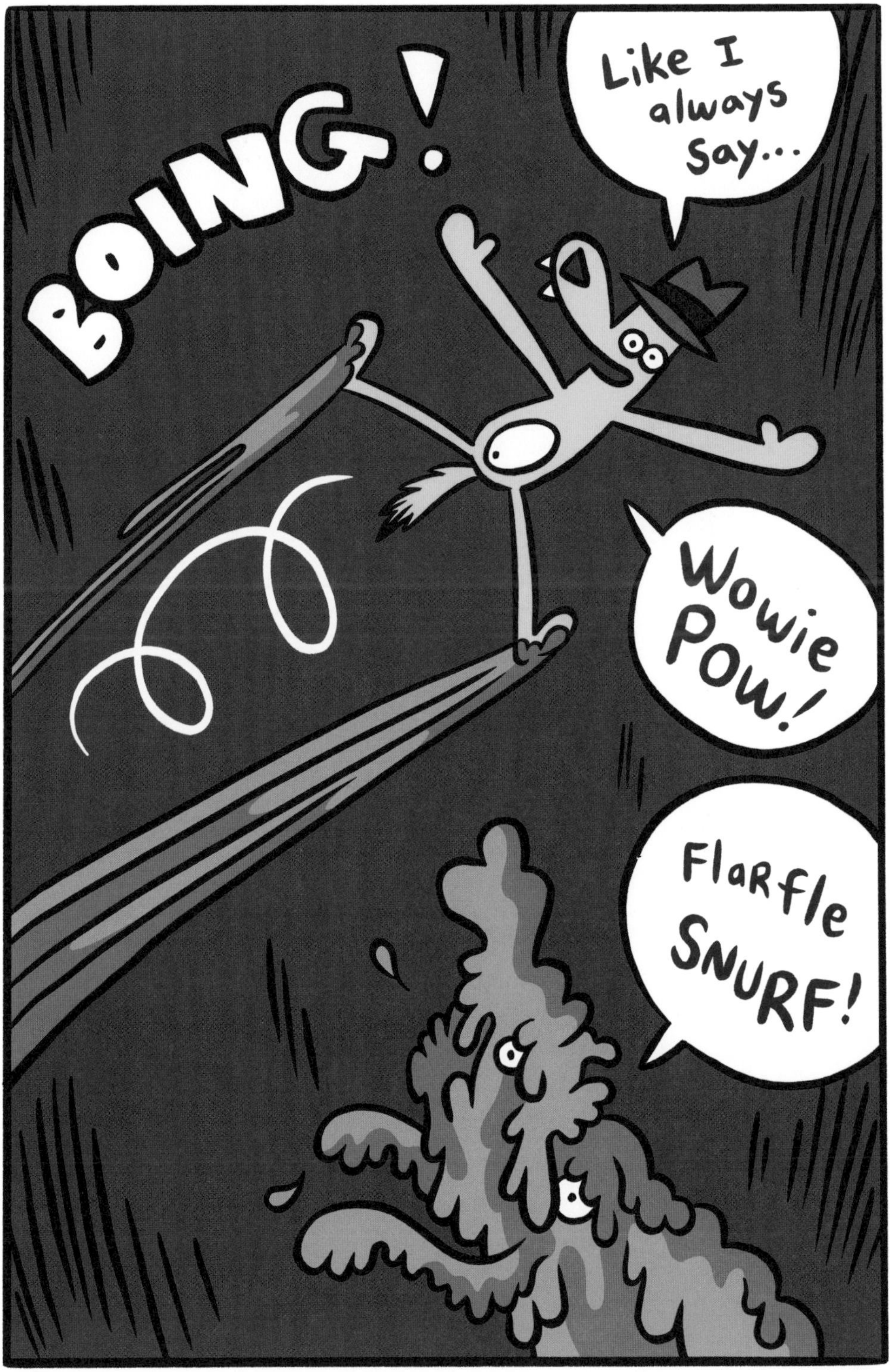
BOING!
Like I always say...
Wowie Pow!
Flarfle SNURF!

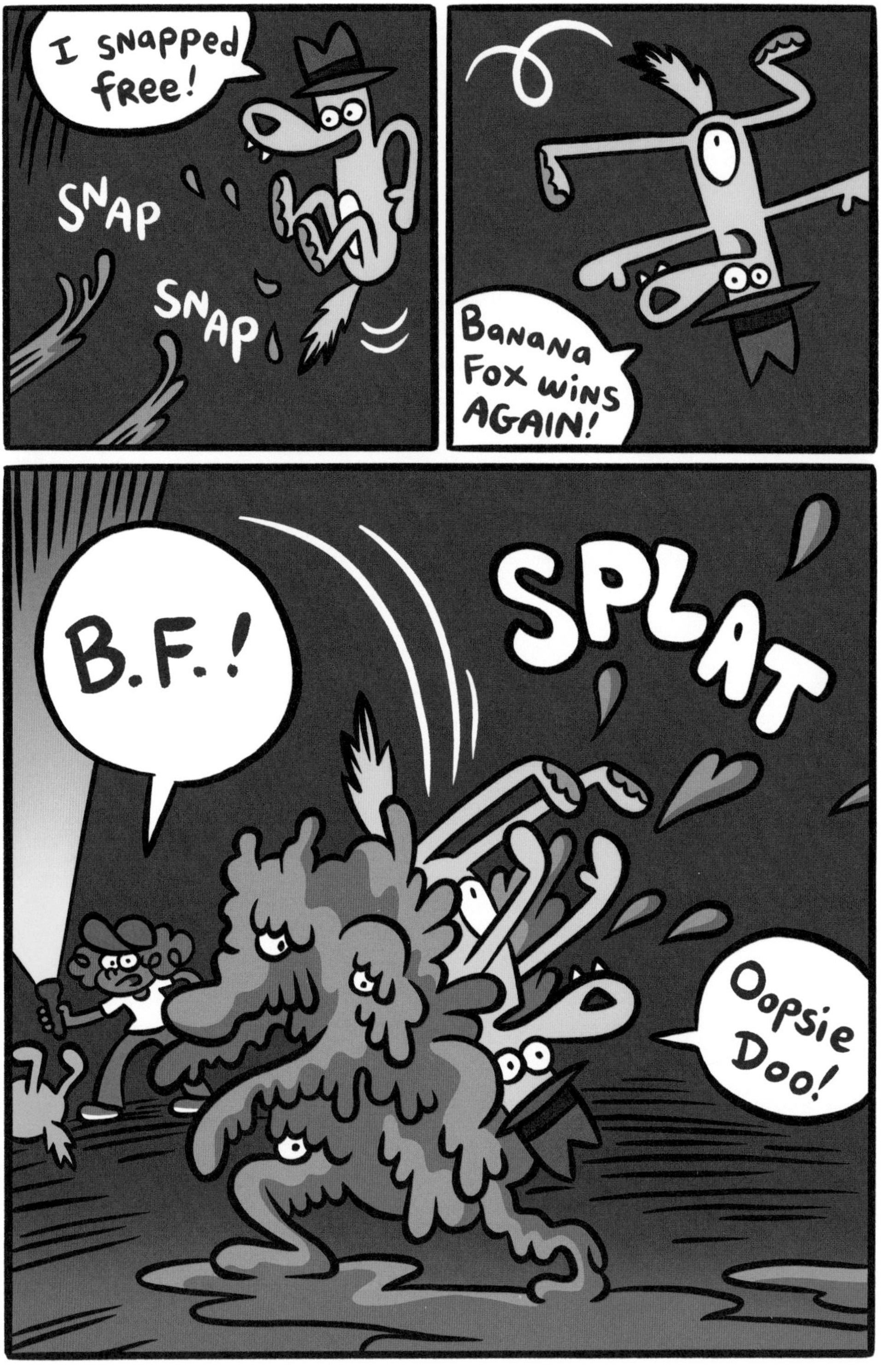
I snapped free!
SNAP
SNAP
Banana Fox wins AGAIN!
B.F.!
SPLAT
Oopsie Doo!

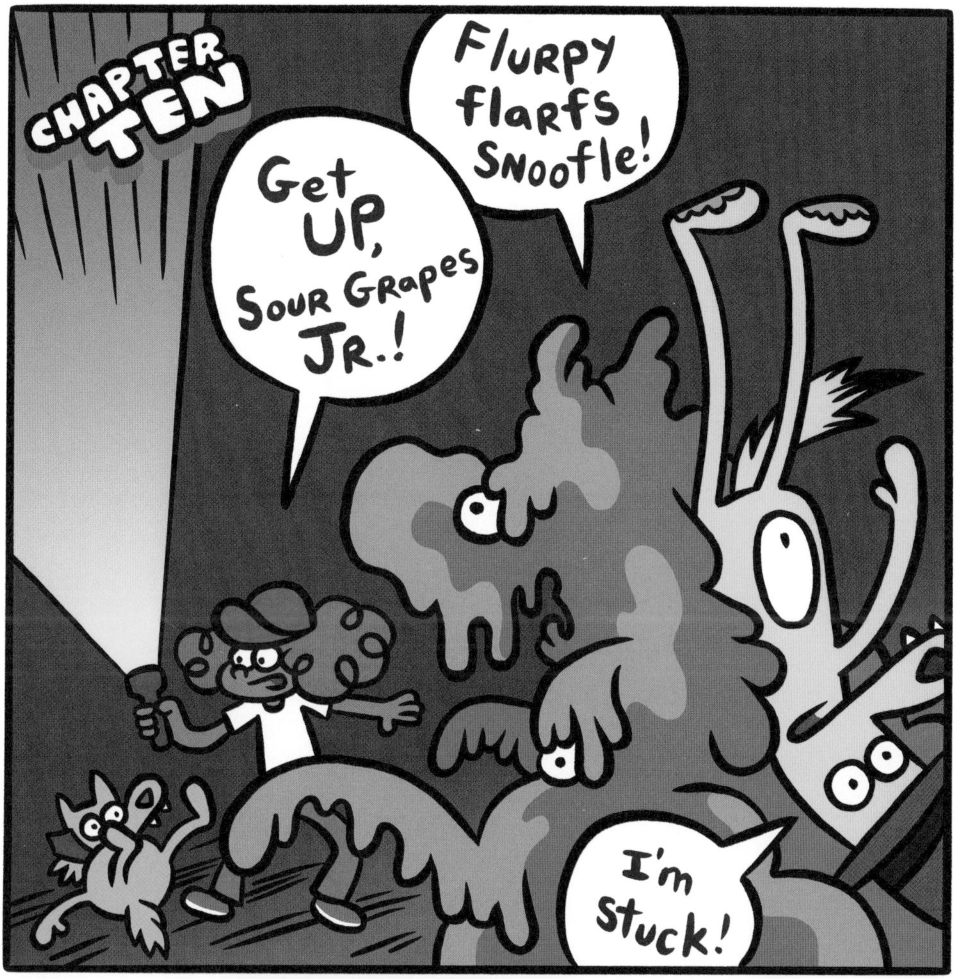
CHAPTER TEN
Get UP, Sour Grapes Jr.!
Flurpy flarfs snoofle!
I'm stuck!

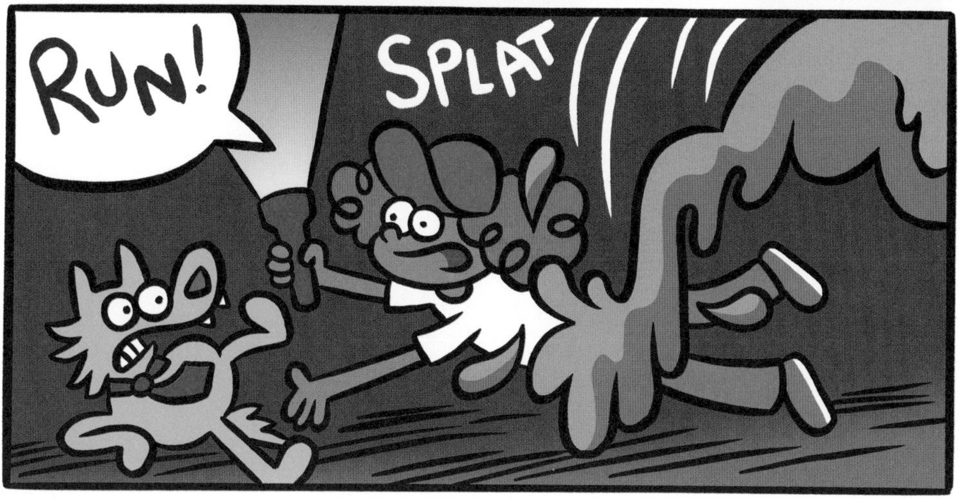
RUN!
SPLAT

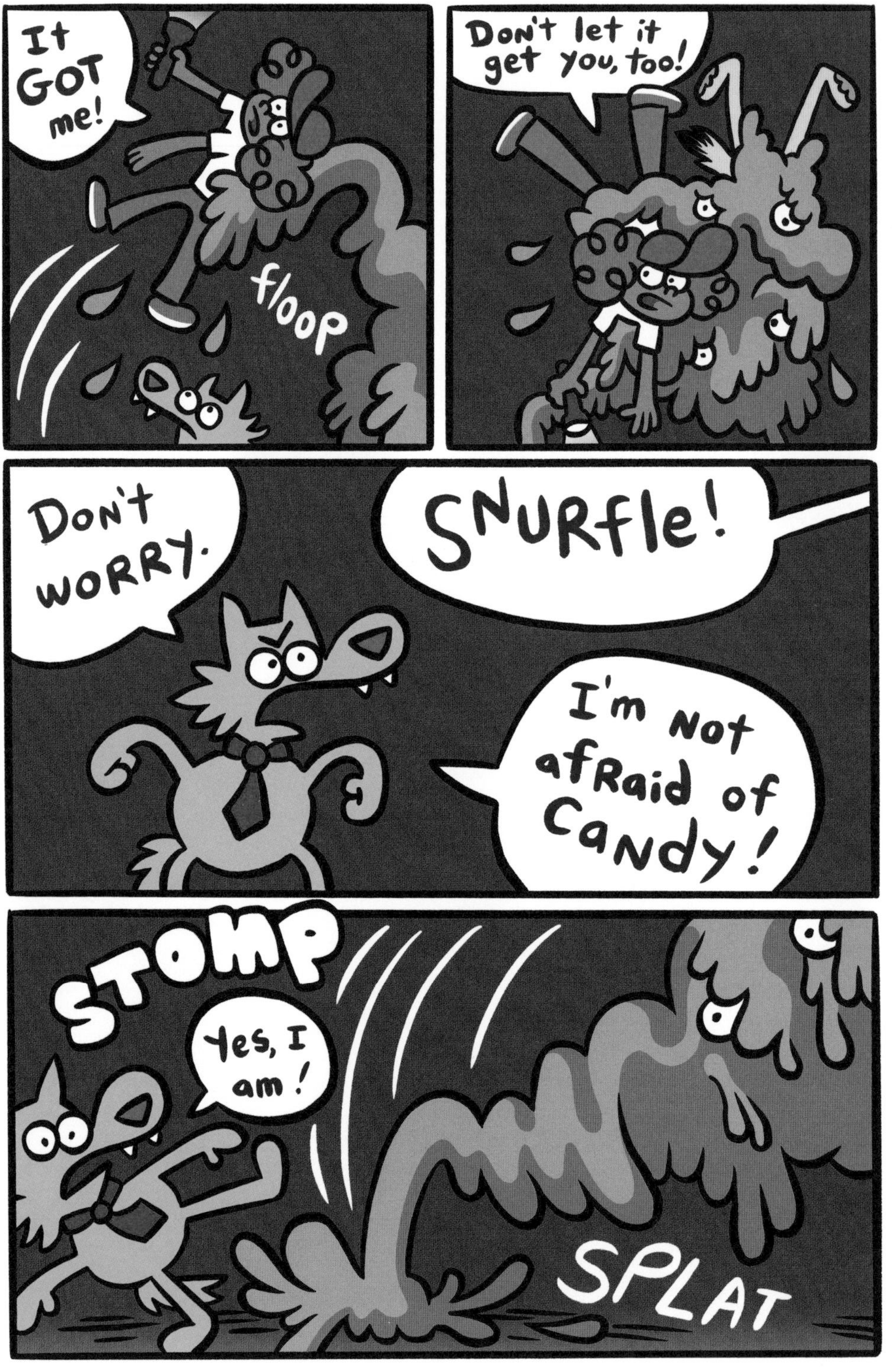
It GOT me!
floop
Don't let it get you, too!
Don't WORRY.
SNURFLE!
I'm NOT afRaid of Candy!
STOMP
Yes, I am!
SPLAT

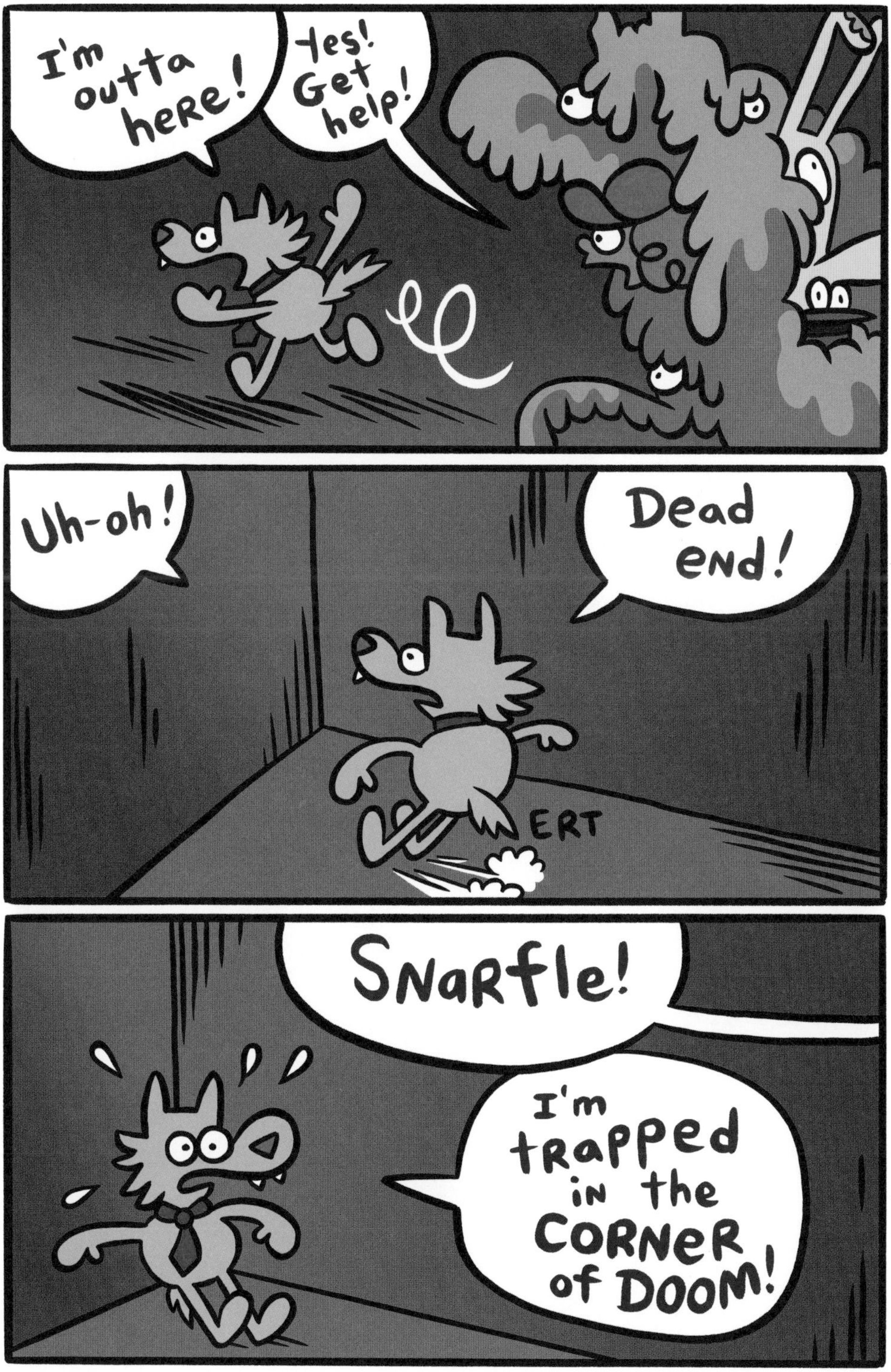
I'm outta here!
Yes! Get help!
Uh-oh!
Dead end!
ERT
Snarfle!
I'm trapped in the CORNER of DOOM!

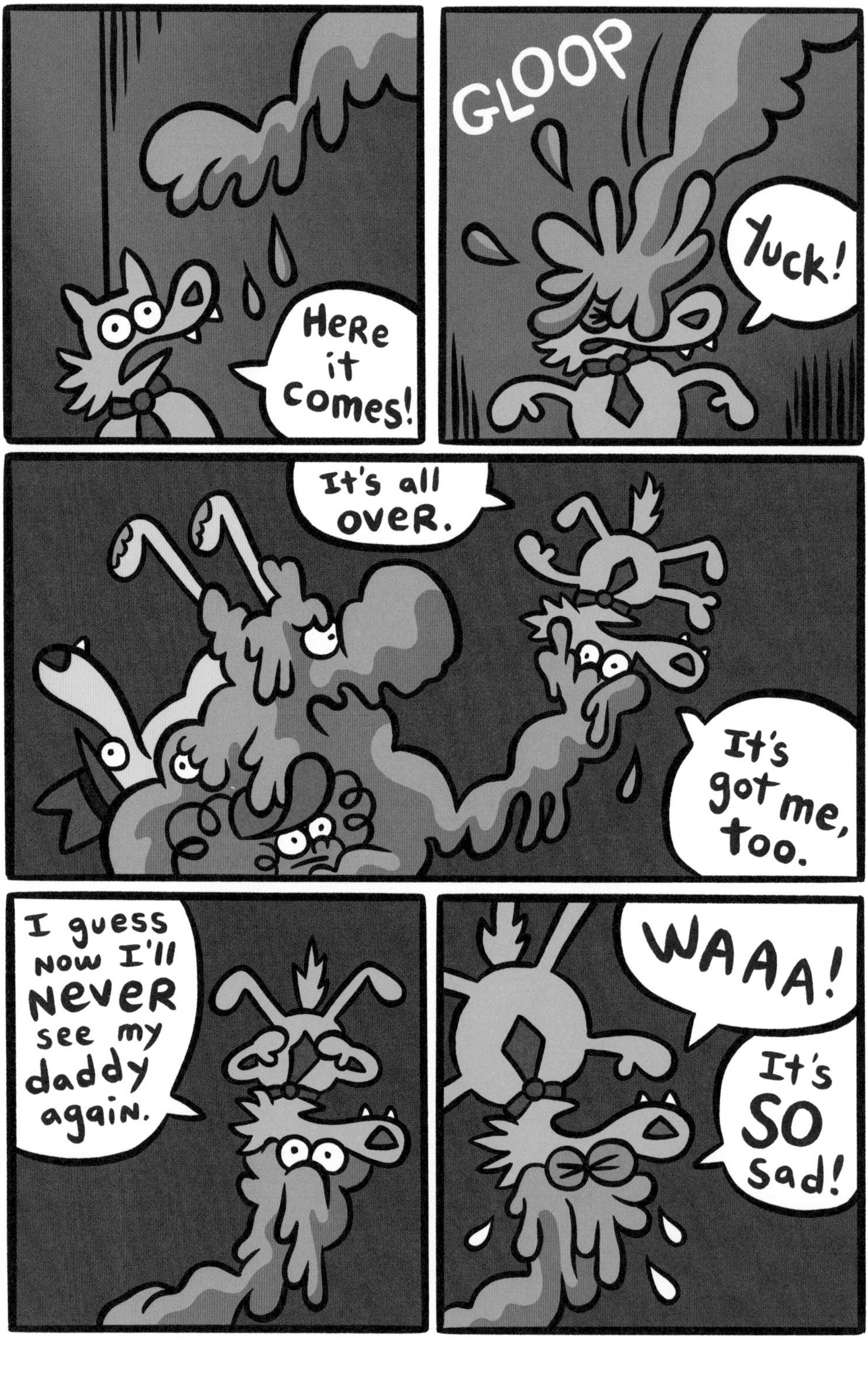
Here it comes!
GLOOP
Yuck!
It's all OVER.
It's got me, too.
I guess now I'll NEVER see my daddy again.
WAAA!
It's SO sad!

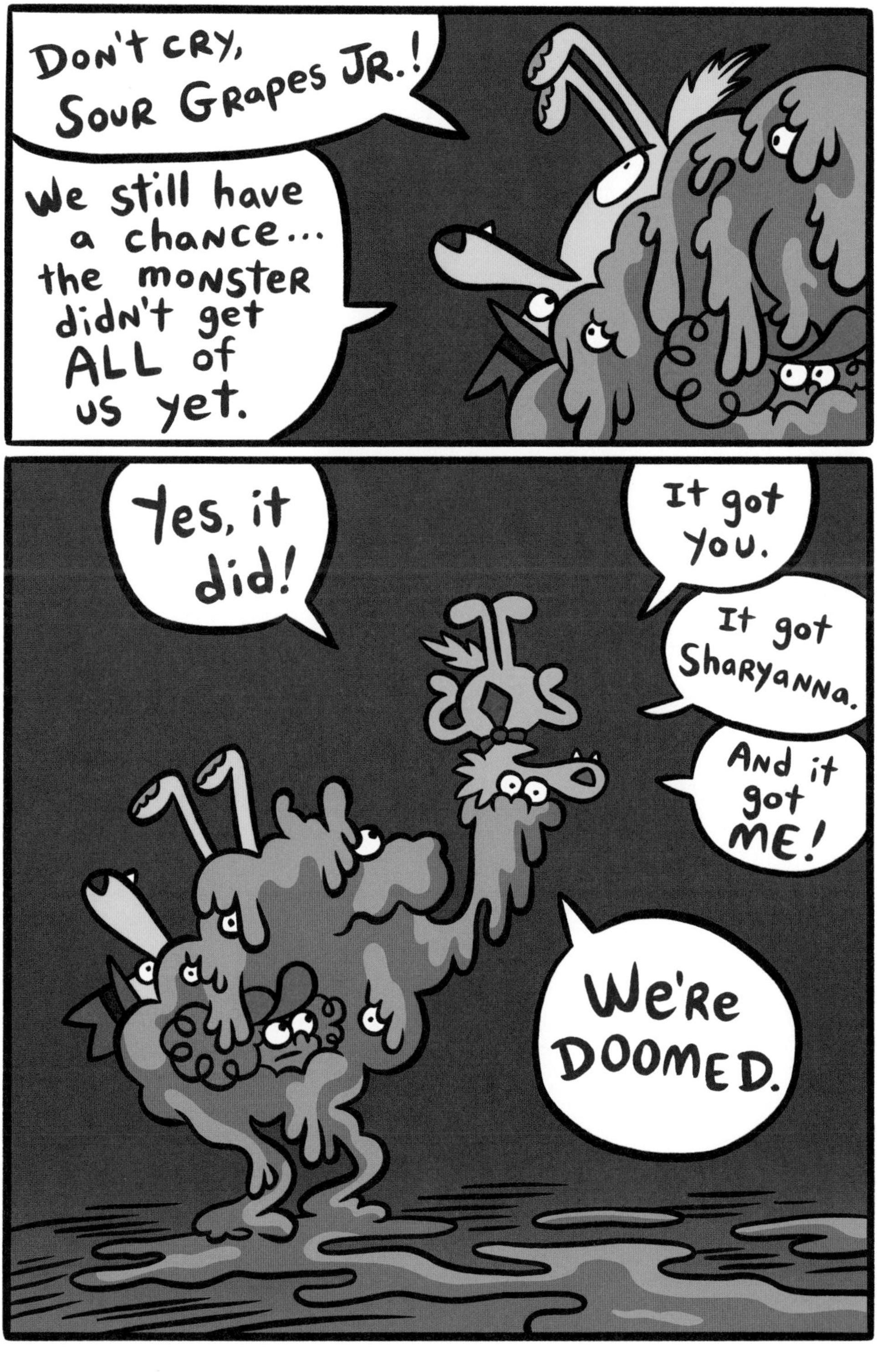
Don't cry, Sour Grapes Jr.!
We still have a chance... the monster didn't get ALL of us yet.
Yes, it did!
It got you.
It got Sharyanna.
And it got ME!
We're DOOMED.

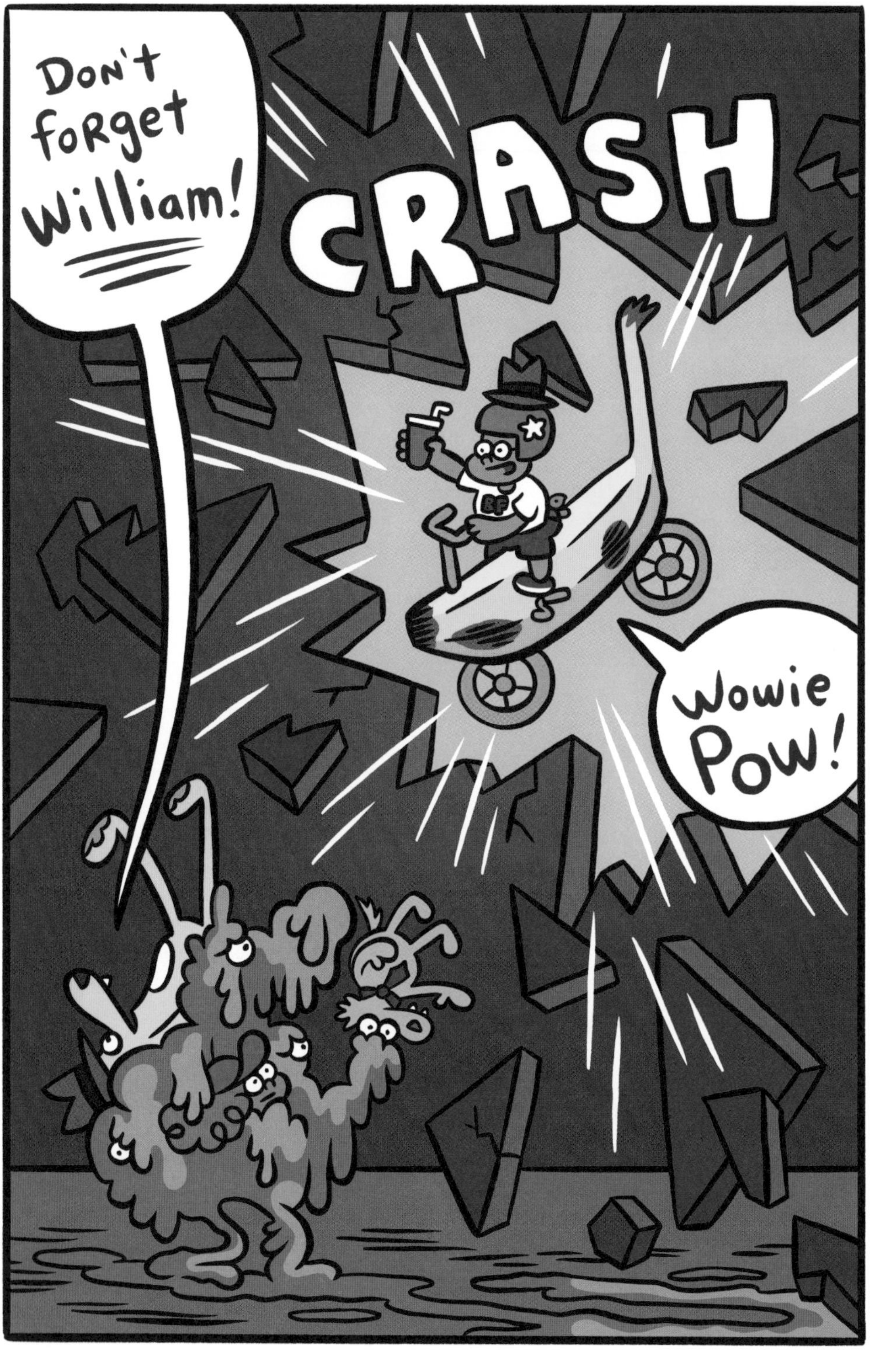
Don't forget William!
CRASH
Wowie Pow!

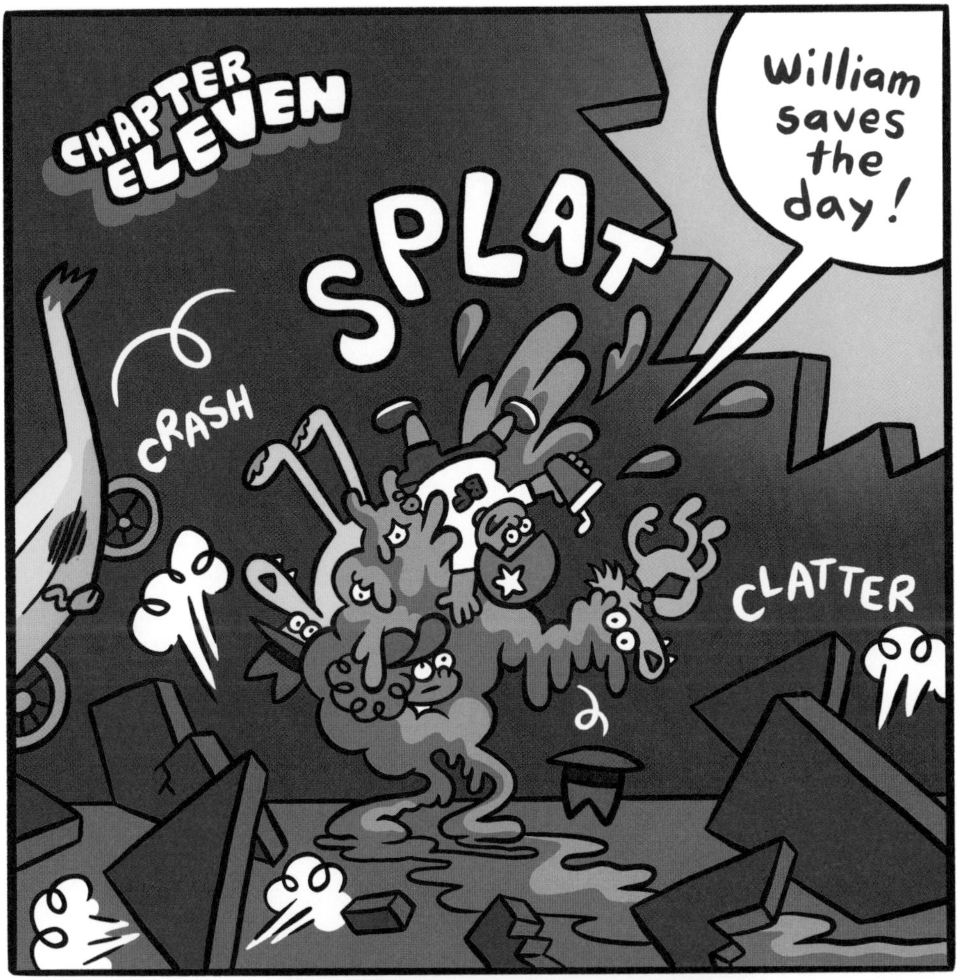
CHAPTER ELEVEN
William saves the day!
SPLAT
CRASH
CLATTER

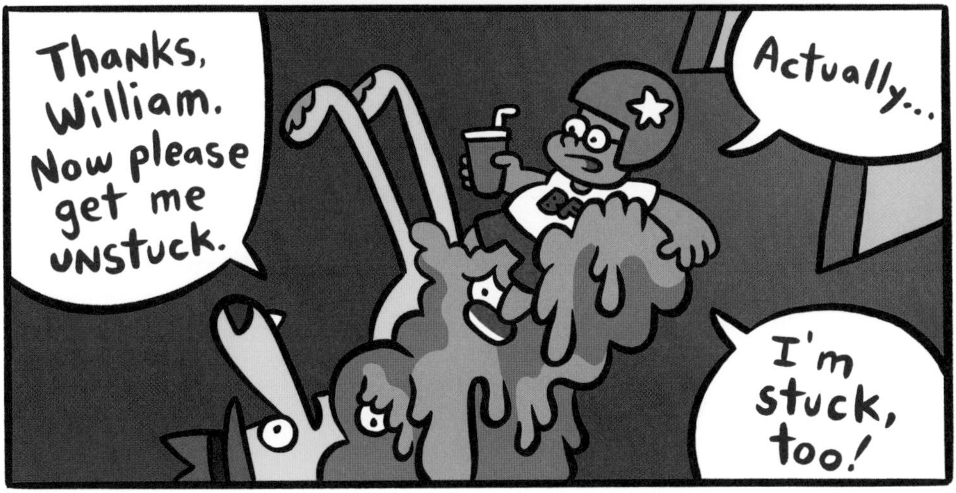
Thanks, William. Now please get me unstuck.
Actually...
I'm stuck, too!

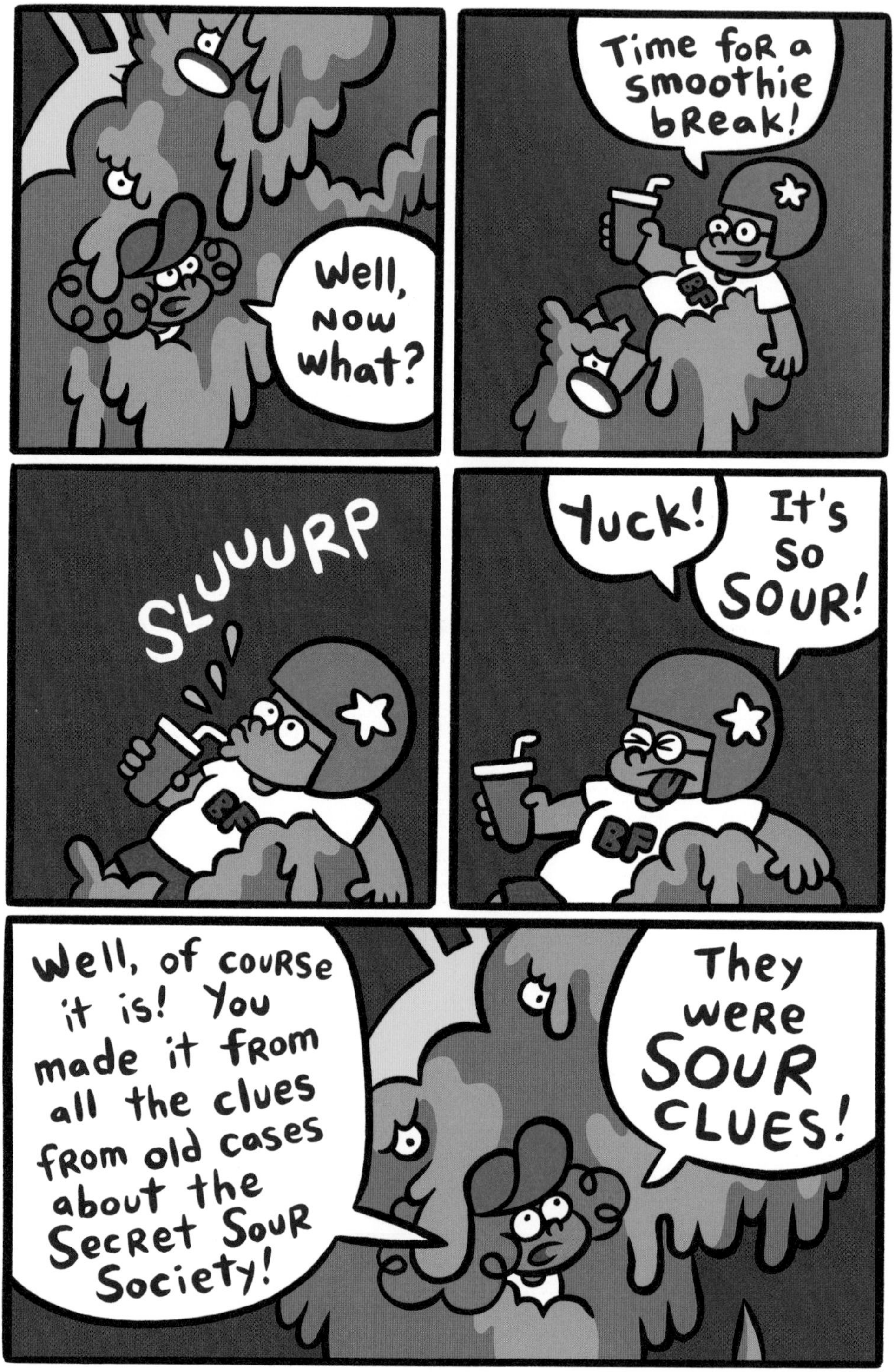
Well, now what?
Time for a smoothie break!
SLUUURP
Yuck!
It's so SOUR!
Well, of course it is! You made it from all the clues from old cases about the Secret Sour Society!
They were SOUR CLUES!

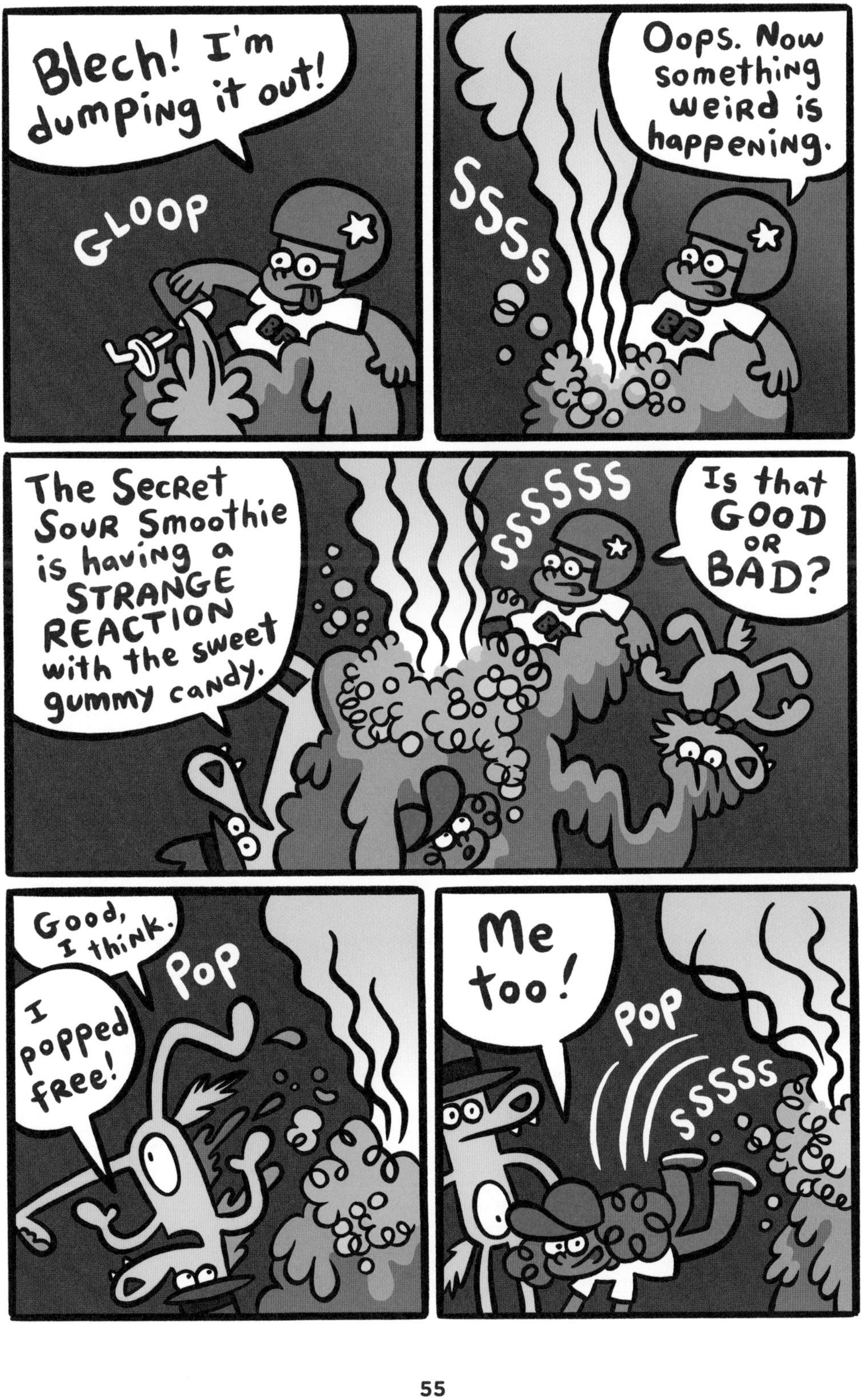
Blech! I'm dumping it out!
GLOOP
Oops. Now something weird is happening.
SSSS
The Secret Sour Smoothie is having a STRANGE REACTION with the sweet gummy candy.
SSSSSS
Is that GOOD OR BAD?
Good, I think.
POP
I popped free!
Me too!
POP
SSSSS

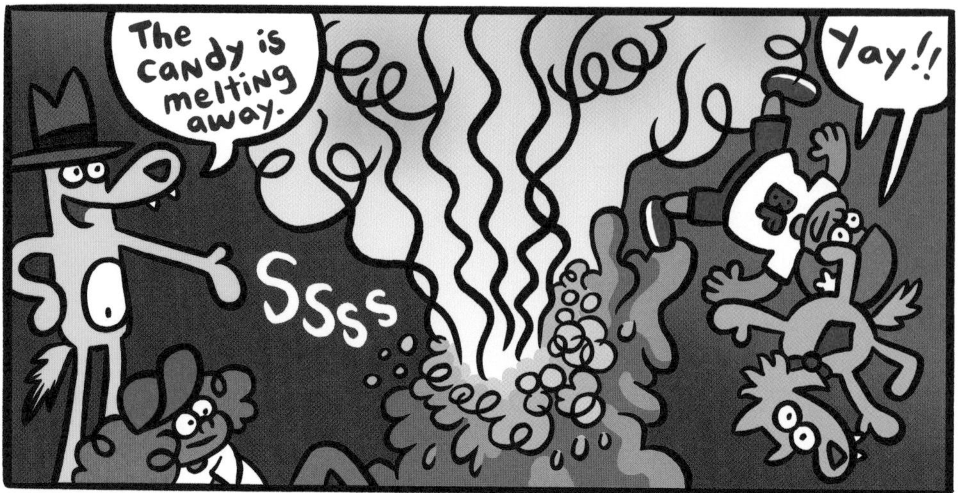
The candy is melting away.
Yay!!
Ssss

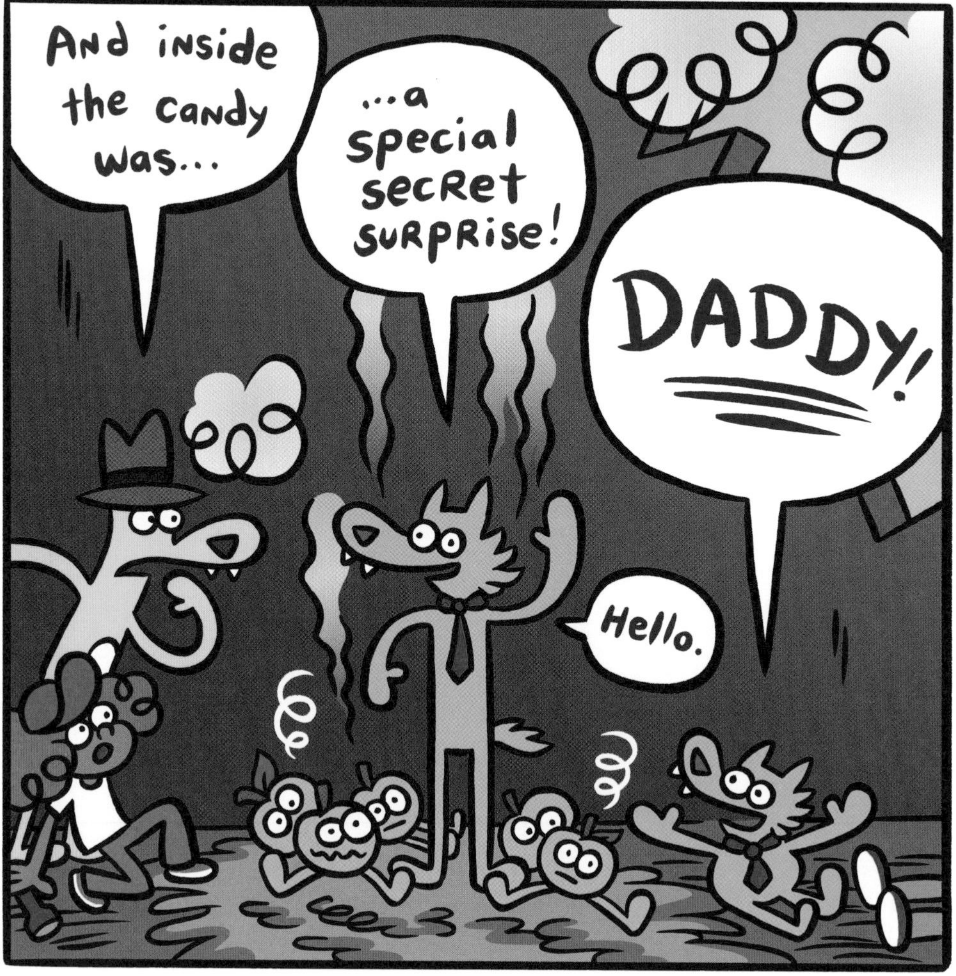
And inside the candy was...
...a special secret surprise!
DADDY!
Hello.

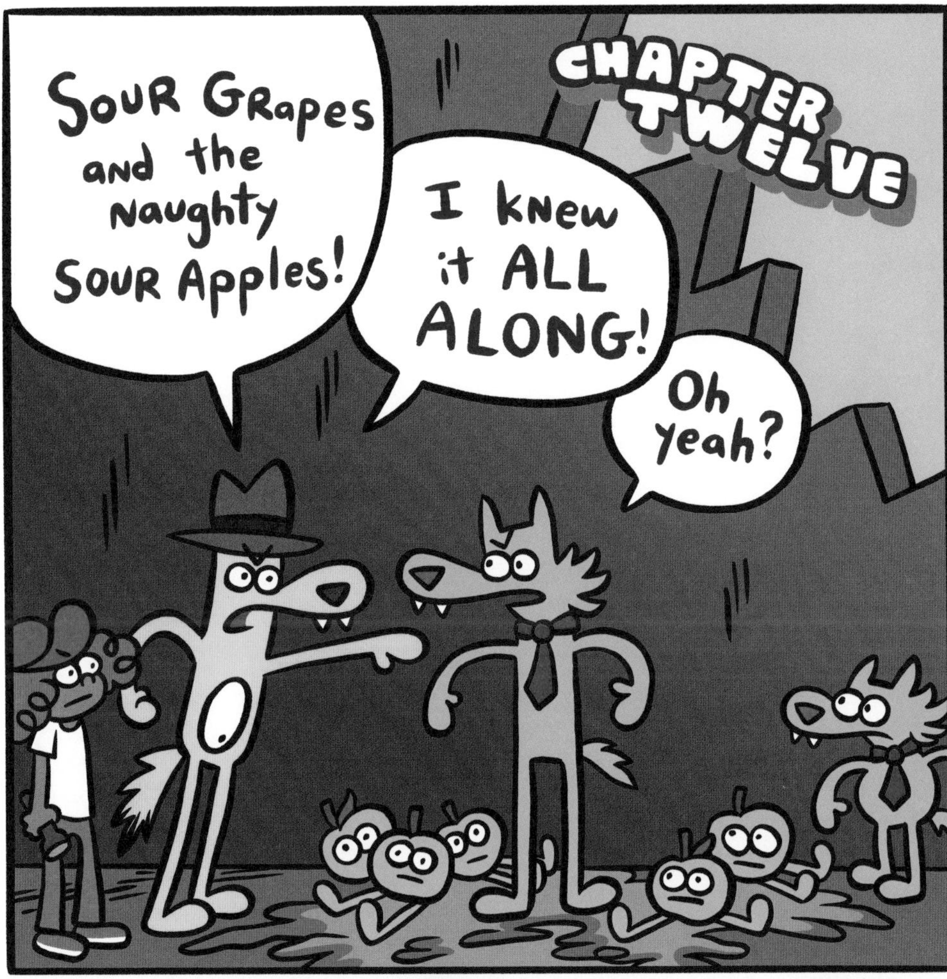
CHAPTER TWELVE
SOUR GRapes and the Naughty SOUR Apples!
I knew it ALL ALONG!
Oh yeah?

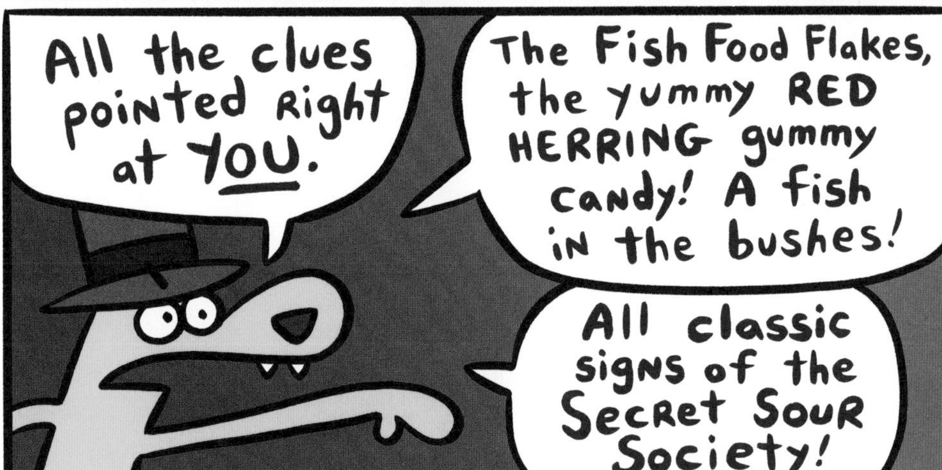
All the clues pointed Right at YOU.
The Fish Food Flakes, the yummy RED HERRING gummy candy! A fish in the bushes!
All classic signs of the Secret SouR Society!

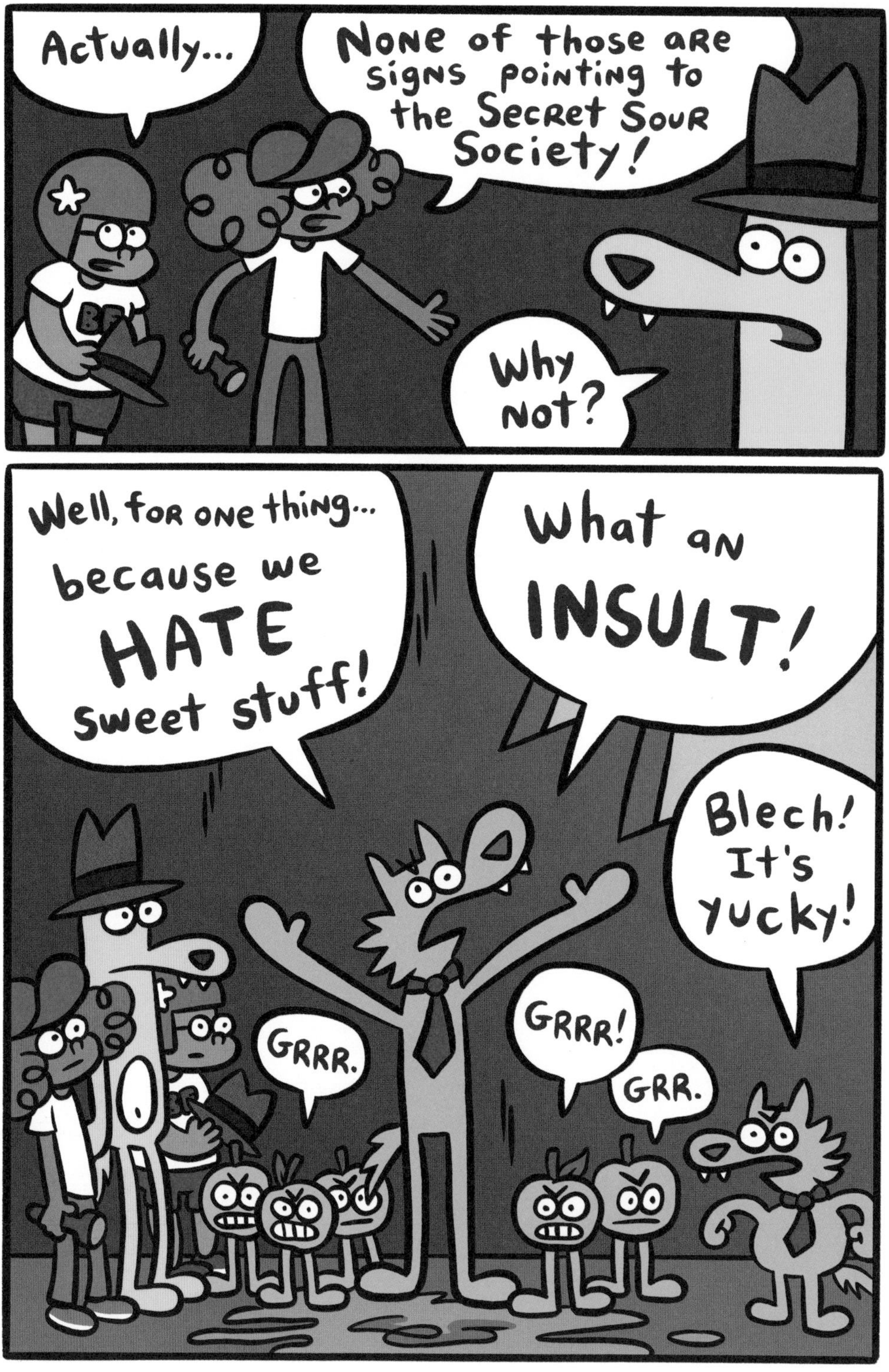
Actually...
None of those are signs pointing to the Secret Sour Society!
Why not?
Well, for one thing... because we HATE sweet stuff!
What an INSULT!
Blech! It's yucky!
GRRR.
GRRR!
GRR.

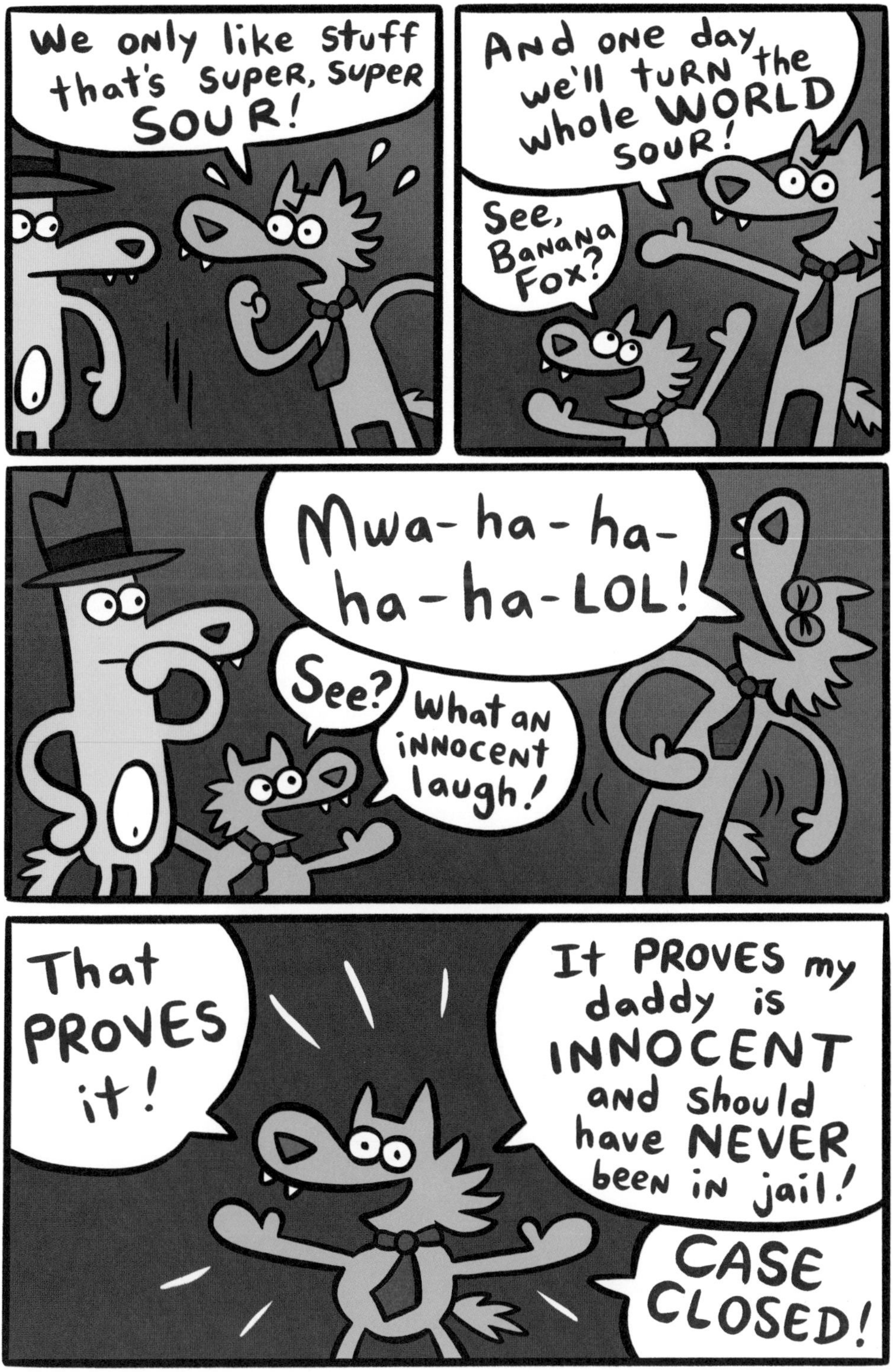
We only like stuff that's SUPER, SUPER SOUR!
And one day we'll TURN the whole WORLD SOUR!
See, BANANA FOX?
Mwa-ha-ha-ha-ha-LOL!
See?
What AN INNOCENT laugh!
That PROVES it!
It PROVES my daddy is INNOCENT and should have NEVER been in jail!
CASE CLOSED!

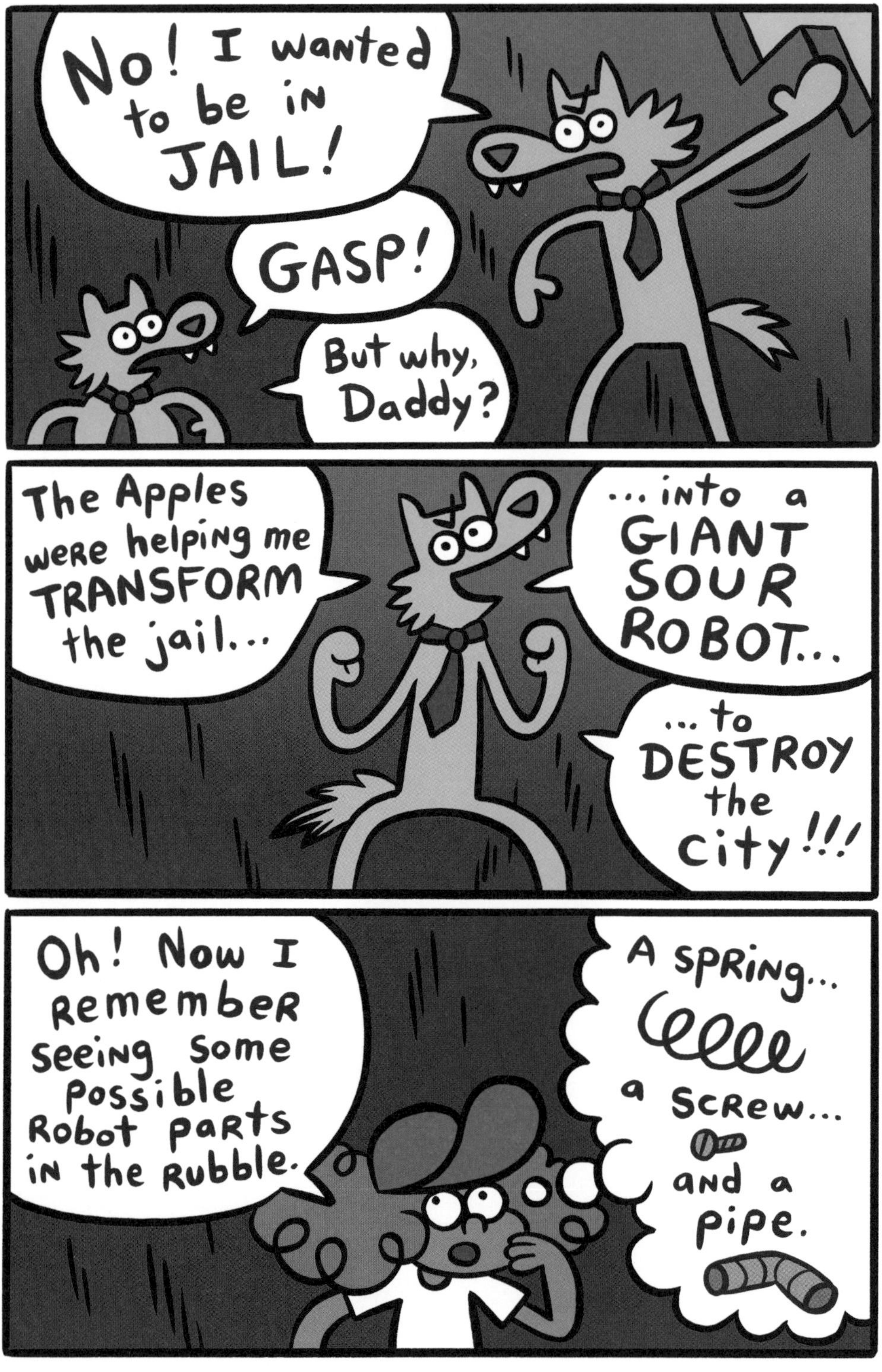

No! I wanted to be in JAIL!
GASP!
But why, Daddy?
The Apples were helping me TRANSFORM the jail...
...into a GIANT SOUR ROBOT...
...to DESTROY the city!!!
Oh! Now I remember seeing some possible Robot parts in the Rubble.
A spring...
a screw...
and a pipe.

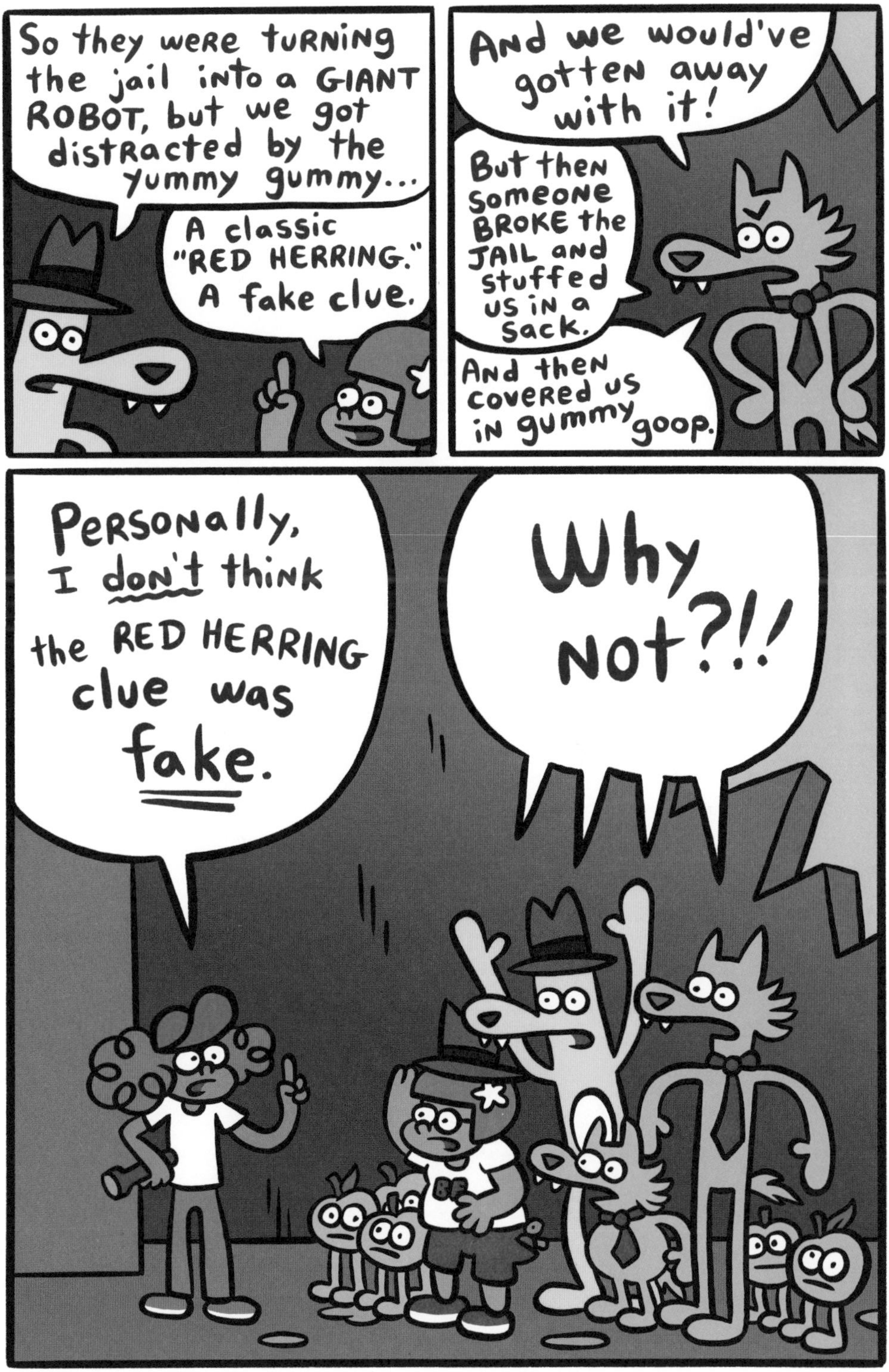
So they were turning the jail into a GIANT ROBOT, but we got distracted by the yummy gummy...
A classic "RED HERRING." A fake clue.
And we would've gotten away with it!
But then someone BROKE the JAIL and stuffed us in a sack.
And then covered us in gummy goop.
Personally, I don't think the RED HERRING clue was fake.
Why not?!!

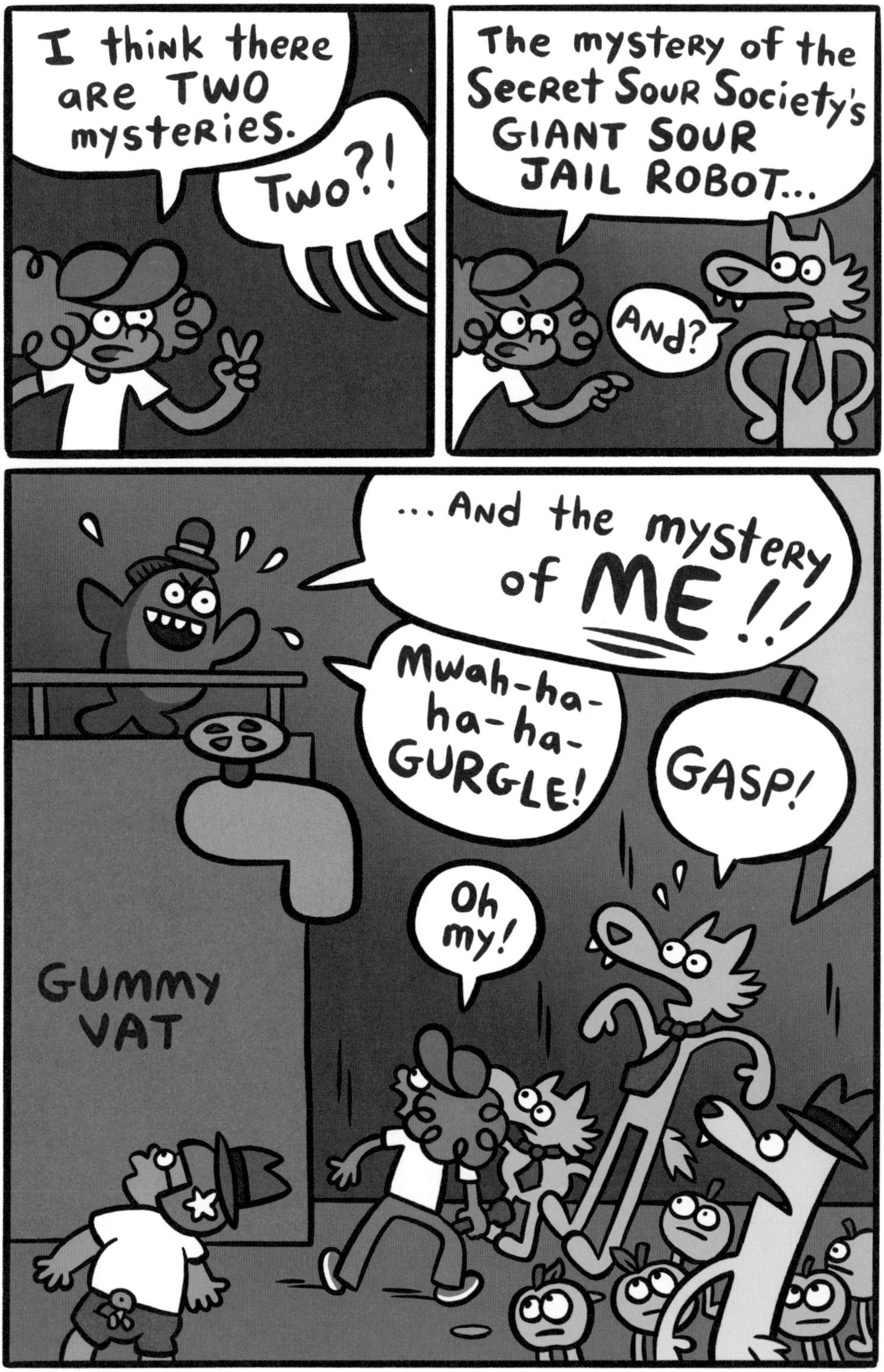
I think there are TWO mysteries.
TWO?!
The mystery of the Secret Sour Society's GIANT SOUR JAIL ROBOT...
AND?
...AND the mystery of ME!!
Mwah-ha-ha-ha-GURGLE!
GASP!
Oh my!
GUMMY VAT

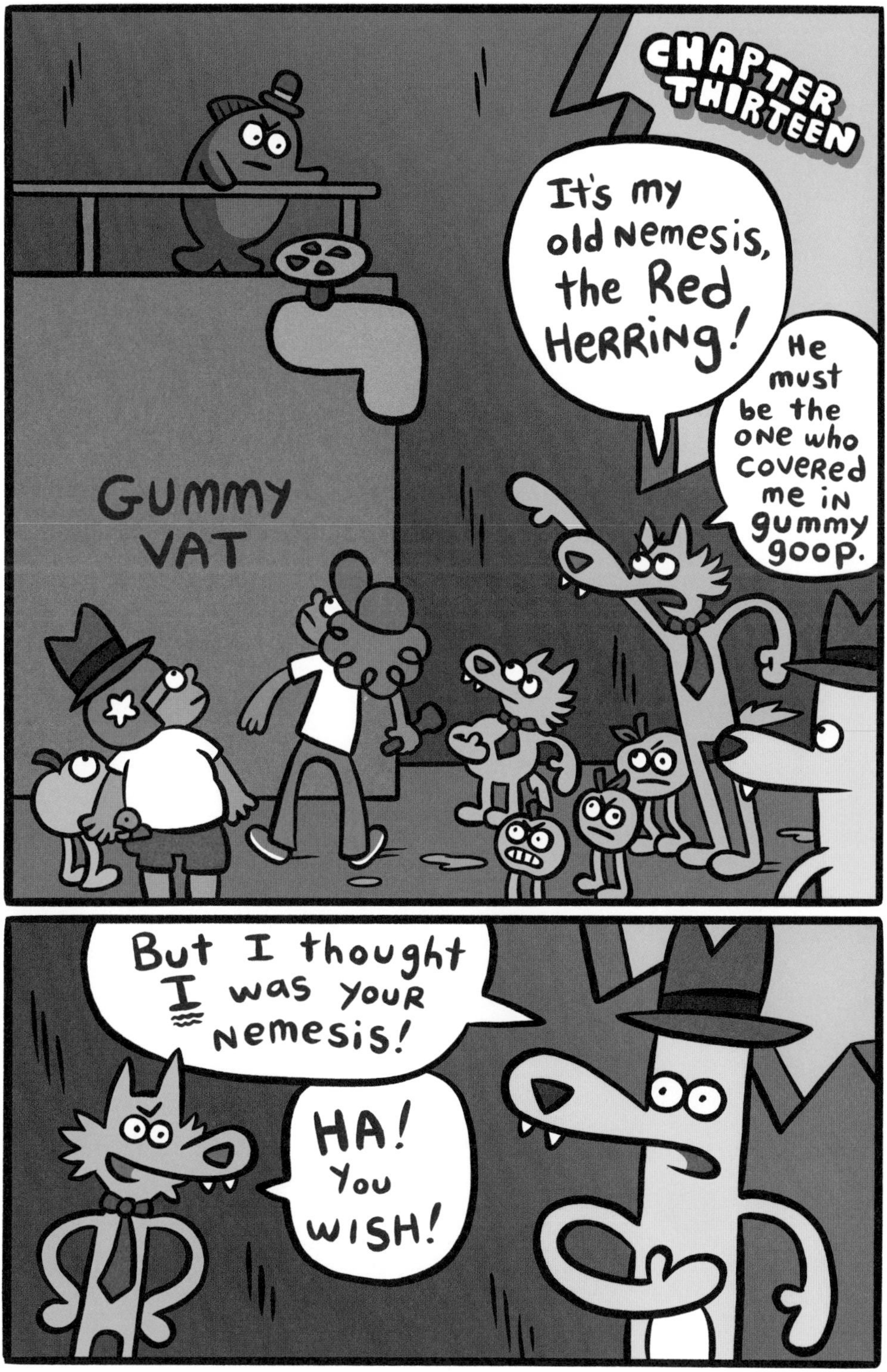
CHAPTER THIRTEEN
GUMMY VAT
It's my old nemesis, the Red Herring!
He must be the one who covered me in gummy goop.
But I thought I was your nemesis!
HA! You WISH!

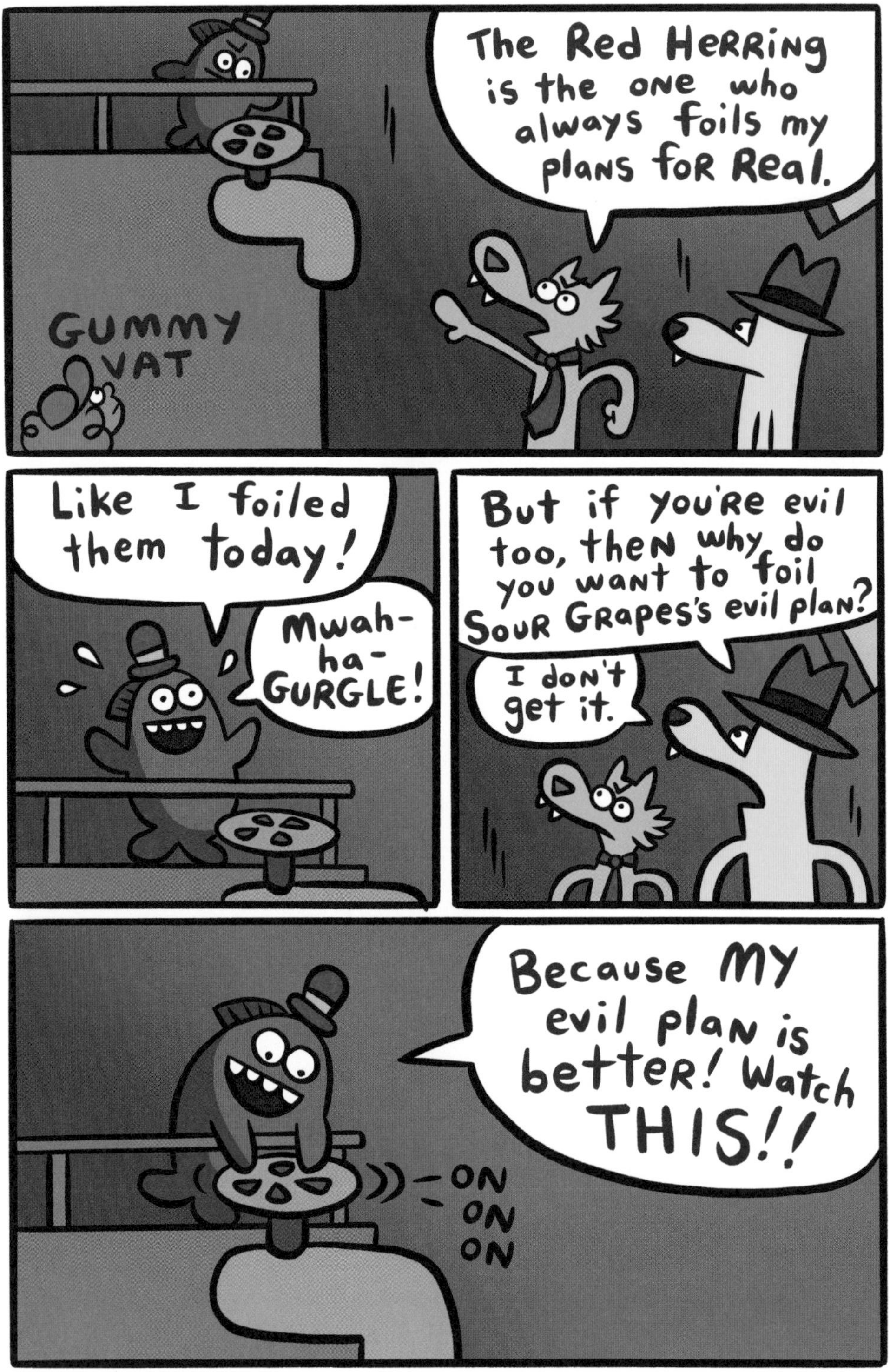
The Red HERRING is the one who always foils my plans for Real.
GUMMY VAT
Like I foiled them today!
Mwah-ha-GURGLE!
But if you're evil too, then why do you want to foil Sour Grapes's evil plan?
I don't get it.
Because MY evil plan is better! Watch THIS!!
ON ON ON

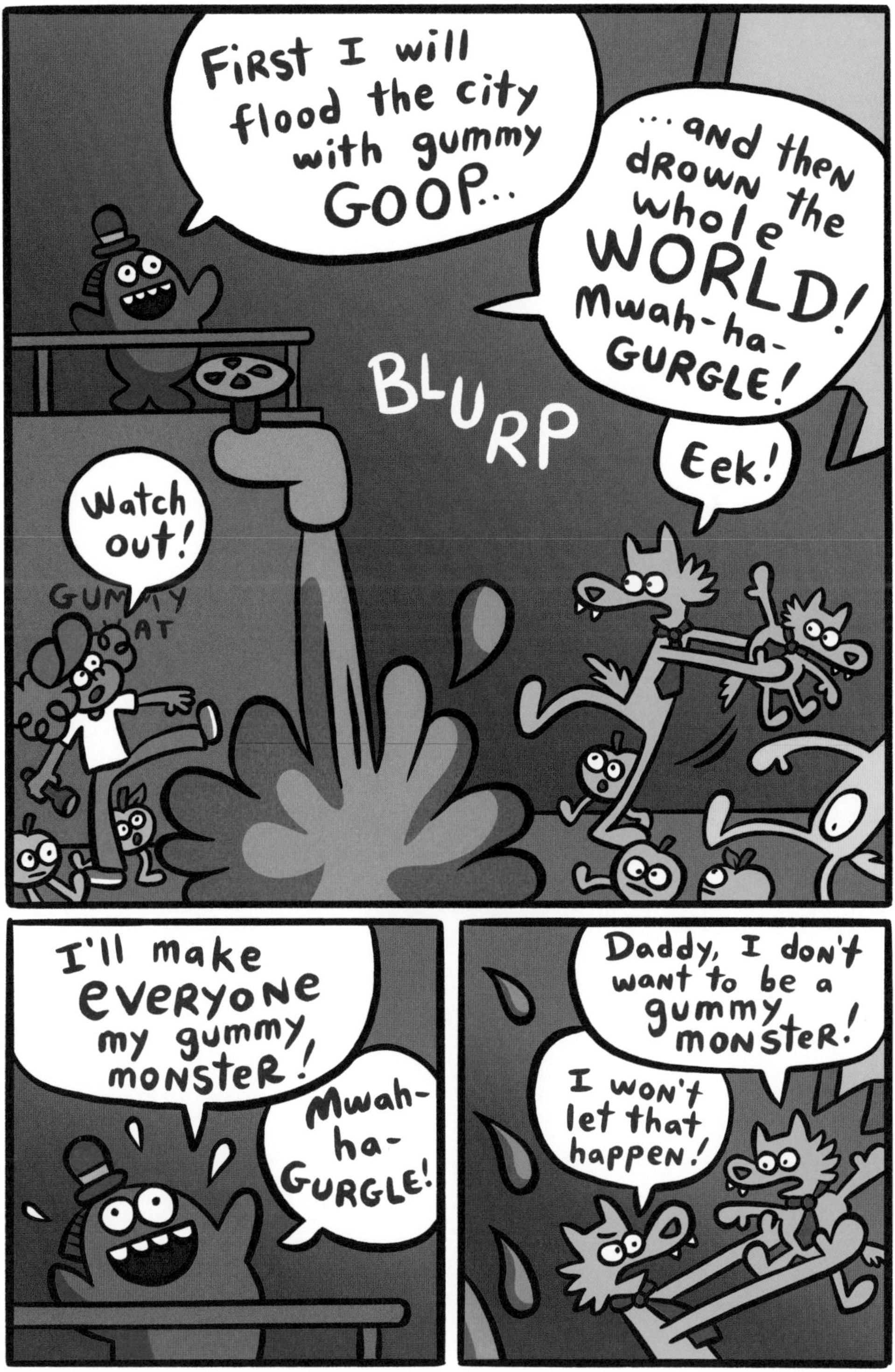

First I will flood the city with gummy GOOP...
...and then drown the whole WORLD! Mwah-ha-GURGLE!
BLURP
Watch out!
Eek!
I'll make EVERYONE my gummy monster!
Mwah-ha-GURGLE!
Daddy, I don't want to be a gummy monster!
I won't let that happen!

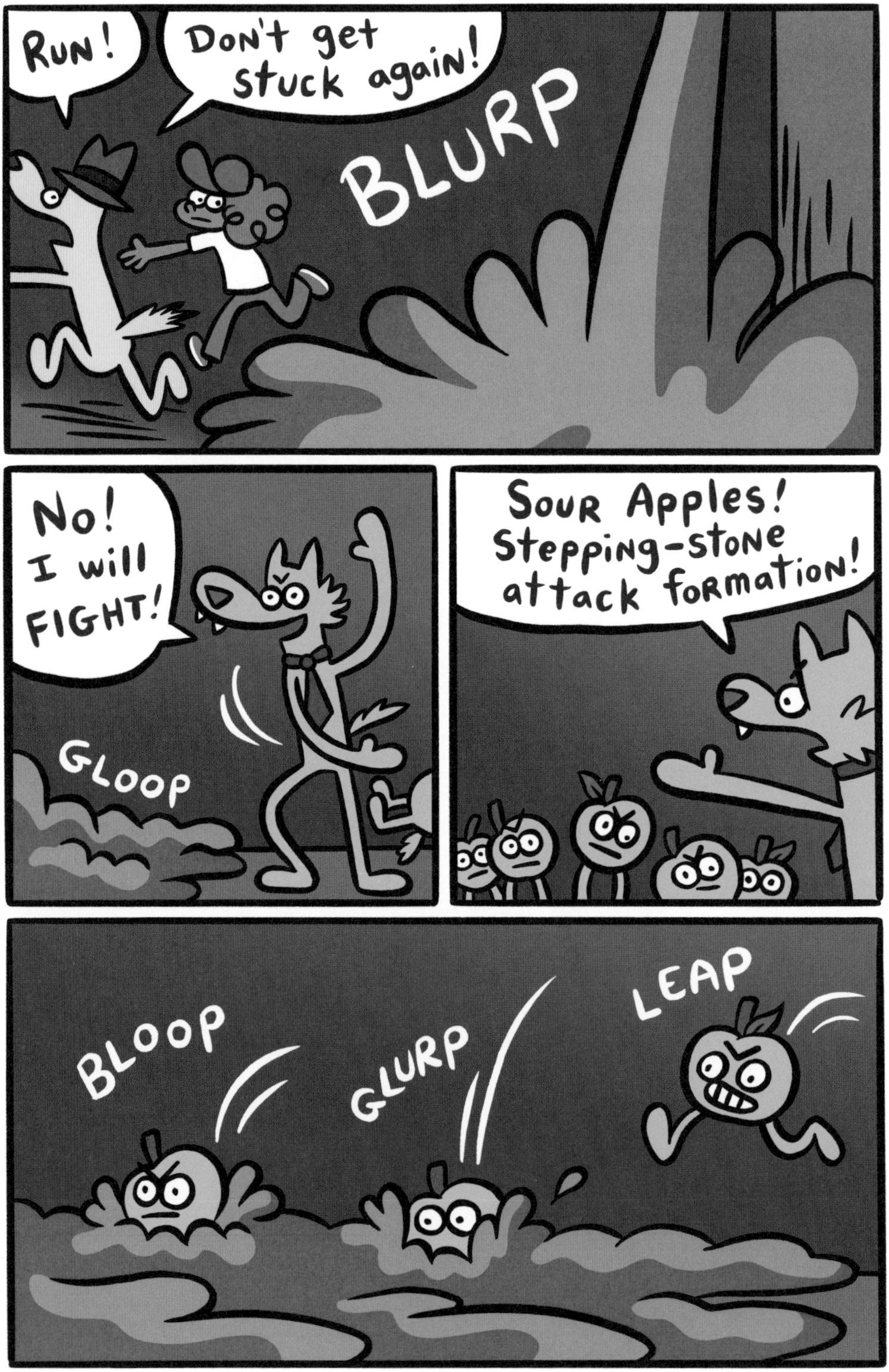

Run!
Don't get stuck again!
BLURP
No! I will FIGHT!
GLOOP
Sour Apples! Stepping-stone attack formation!
BLOOP
GLURP
LEAP

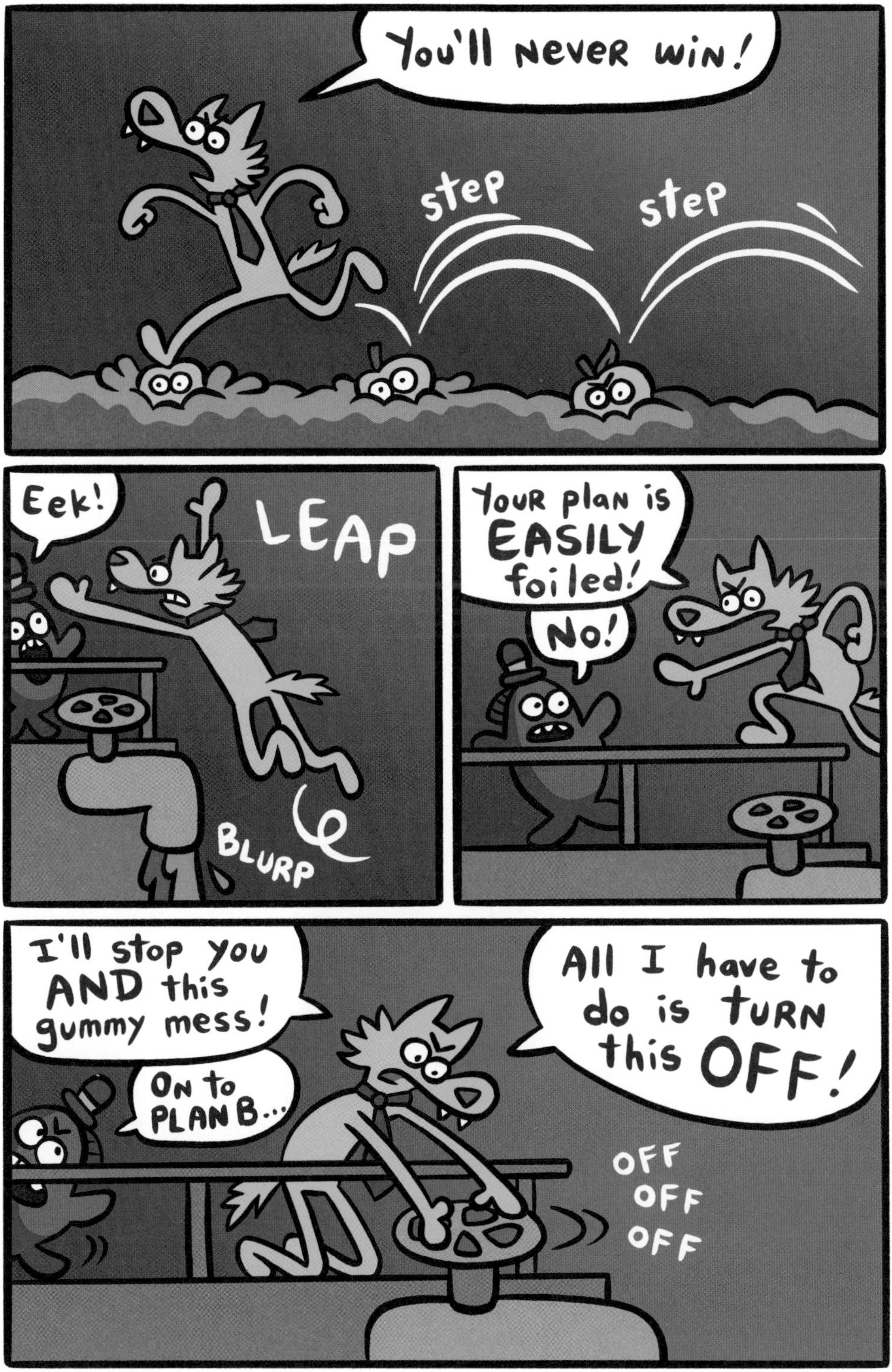
You'll never win!
step
step
Eek!
LEAP
BLURP
Your plan is EASILY foiled!
No!
I'll stop you AND this gummy mess!
On to PLAN B...
All I have to do is TURN this OFF!
OFF
OFF
OFF

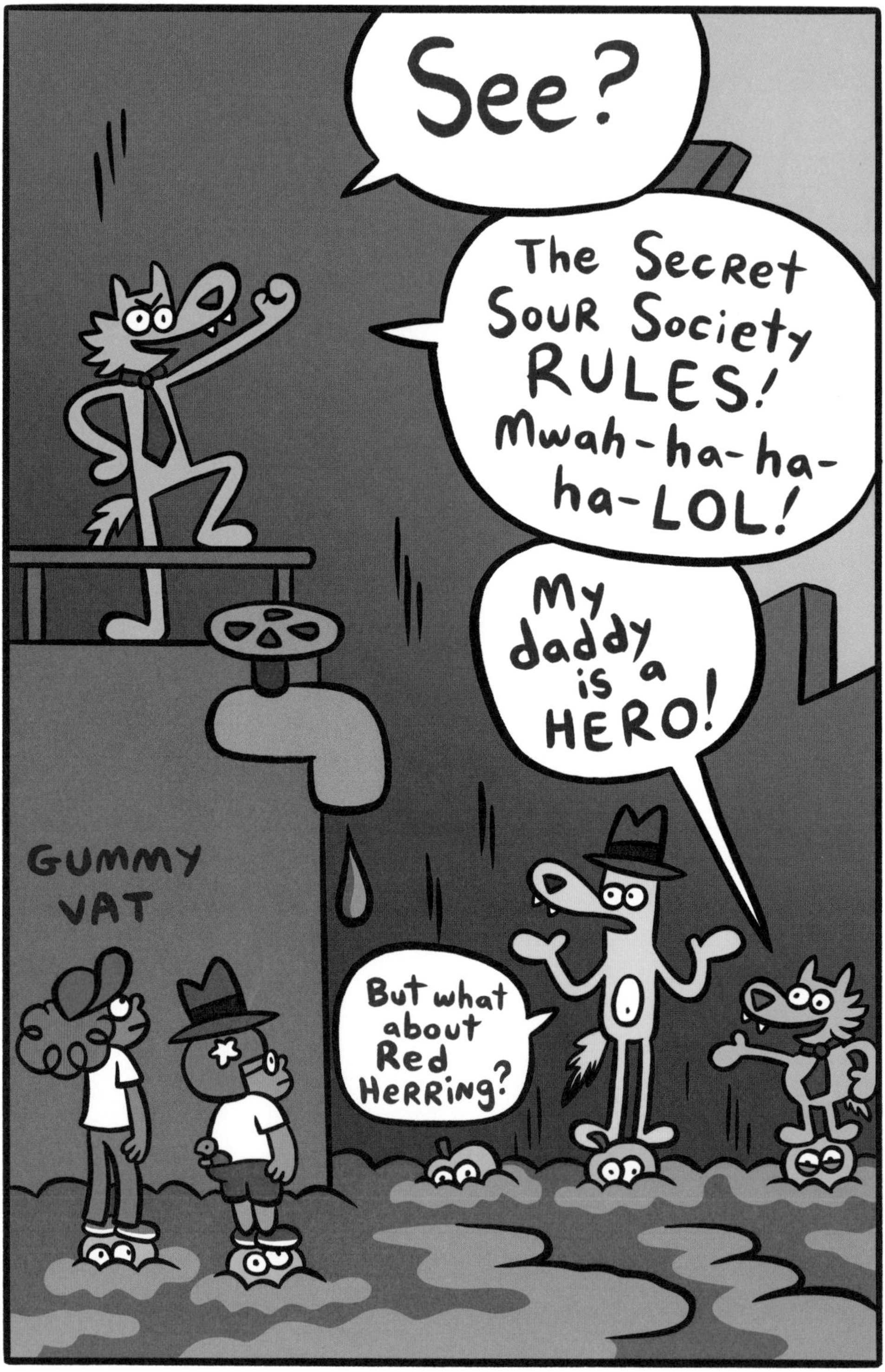
See?
The Secret Sour Society RULES! Mwah-ha-ha-ha-LOL!
My daddy is a HERO!
GUMMY VAT
But what about Red Herring?

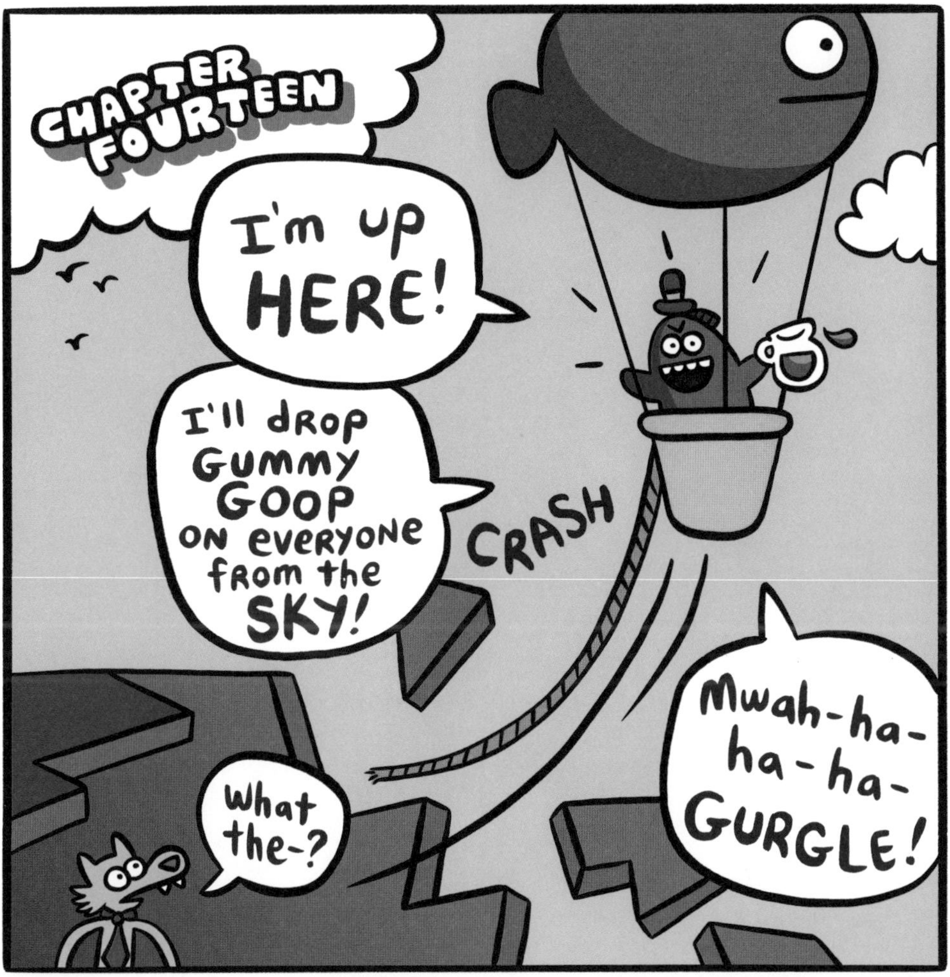
CHAPTER FOURTEEN
I'm up HERE!
I'll drop GUMMY GOOP ON EVERYONE from the SKY!
CRASH
Mwah-ha-ha-ha-GURGLE!
What the-?

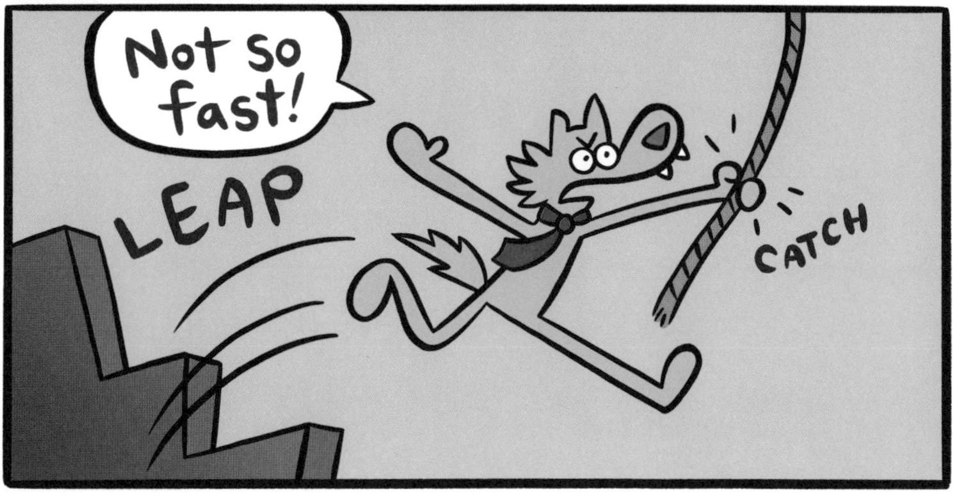
Not so fast!
LEAP
CATCH

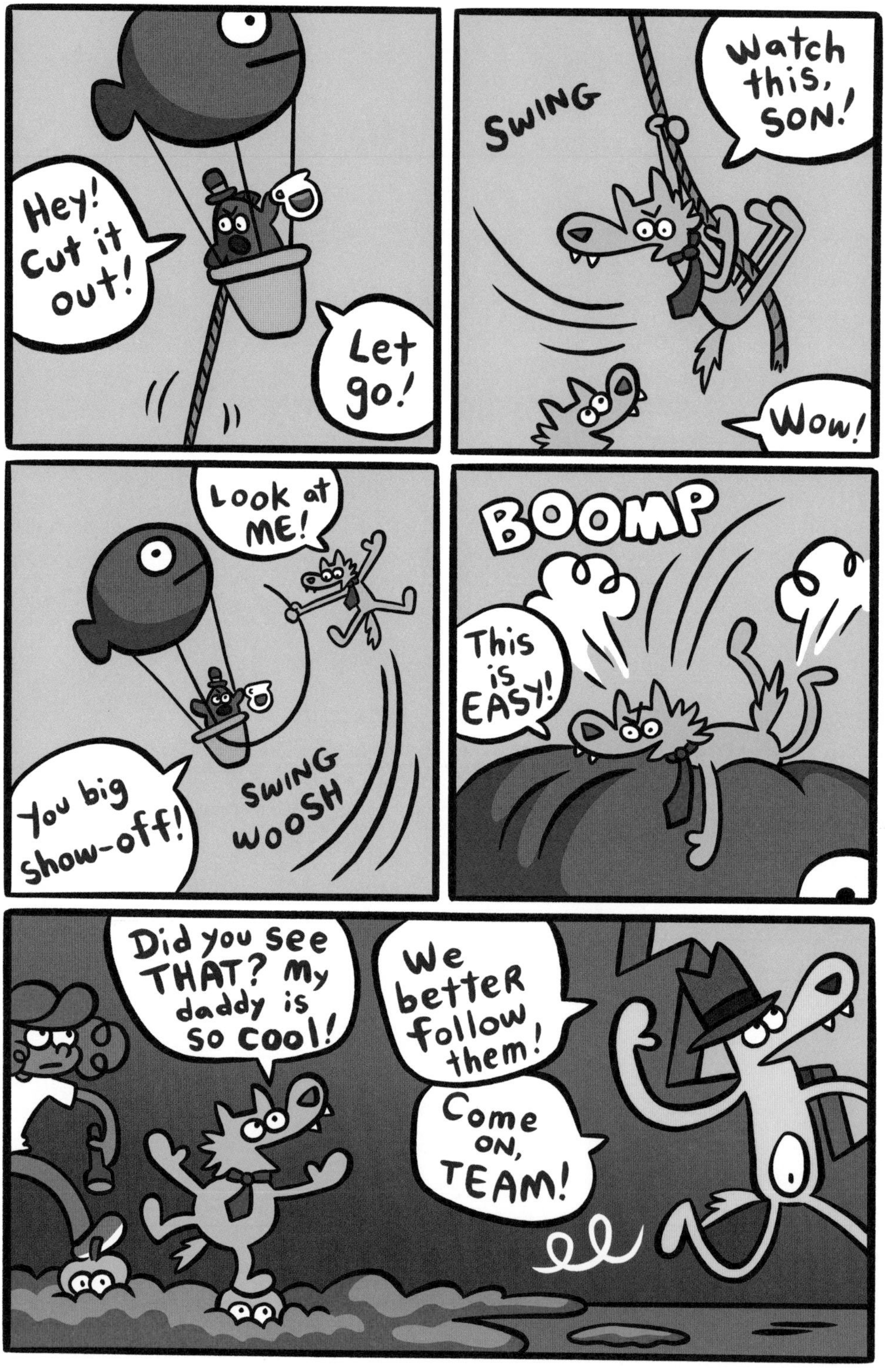
Hey! Cut it out!
Let go!
Watch this, SON!
SWING
Wow!
Look at ME!
You big show-off!
SWING
WOOSH
BOOMP
This is EASY!
Did you see THAT? My daddy is so cool!
We better follow them!
Come ON, TEAM!

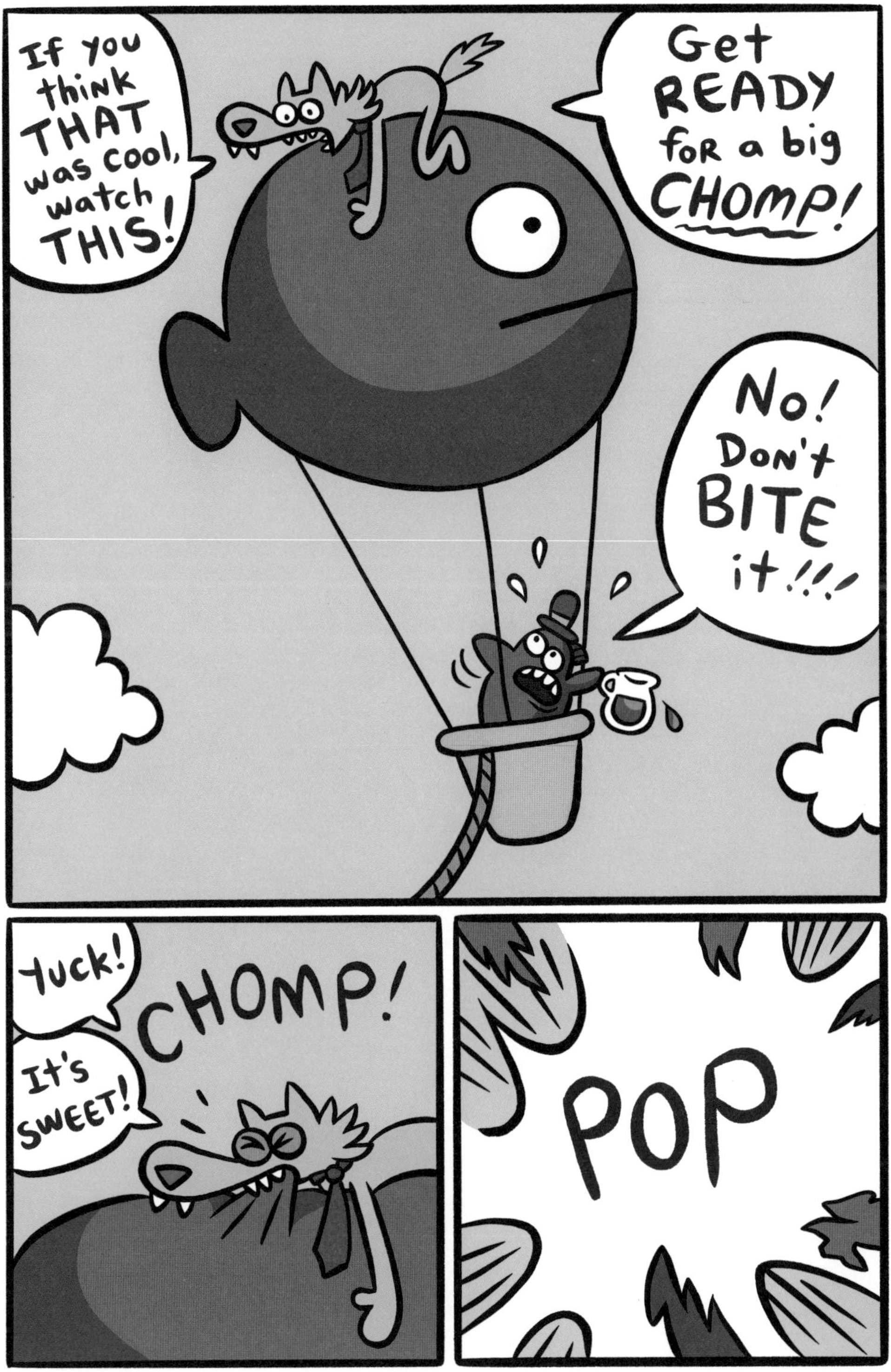
If you think THAT was cool, watch THIS!
Get READY for a big CHOMP!
No! Don't BITE it!!!!
Yuck!
It's SWEET!
CHOMP!
POP

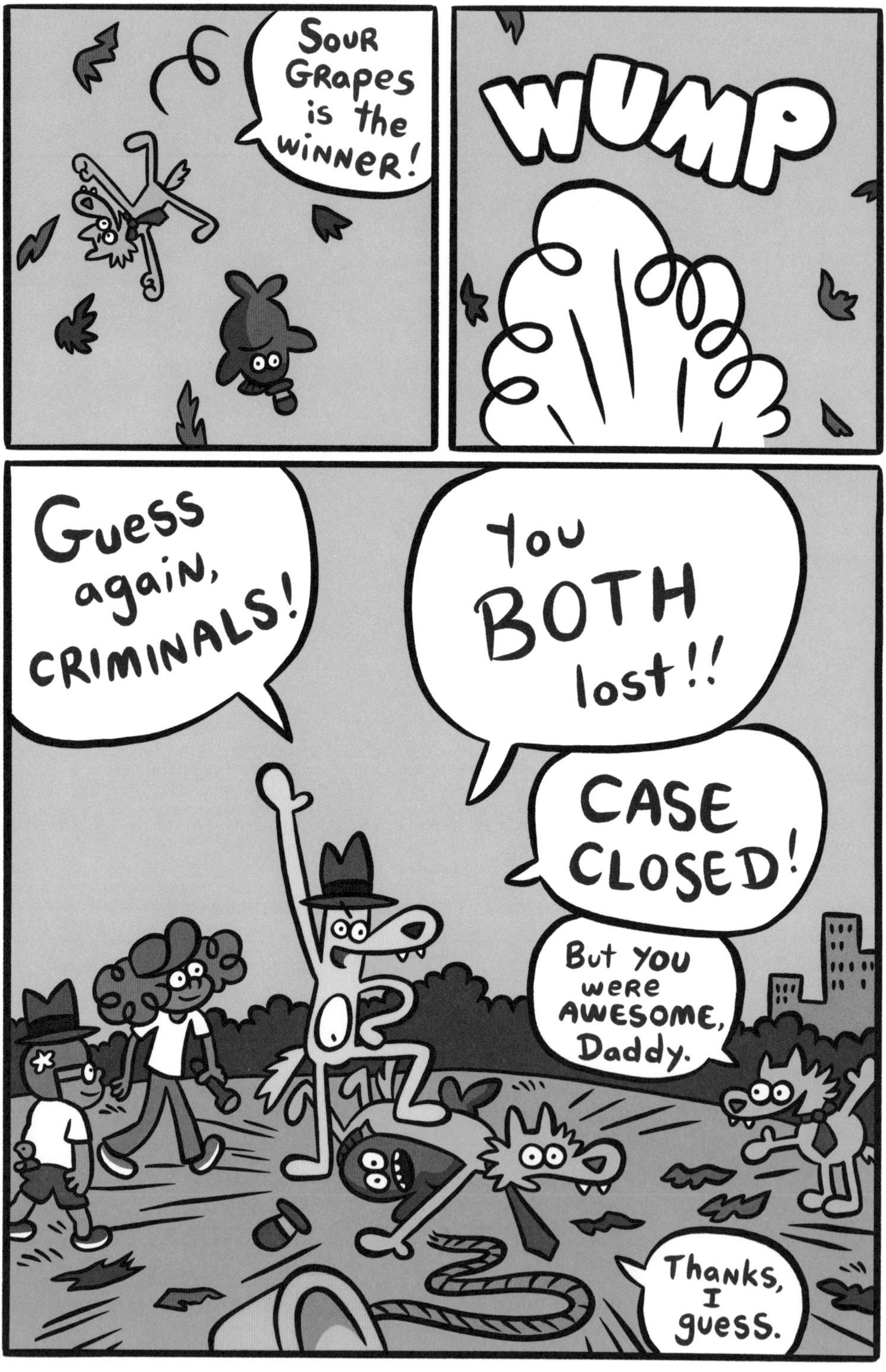
Sour Grapes is the winner!
WUMP
Guess again, CRIMINALS!
You BOTH lost!!
CASE CLOSED!
But you were AWESOME, Daddy.
Thanks, I guess.

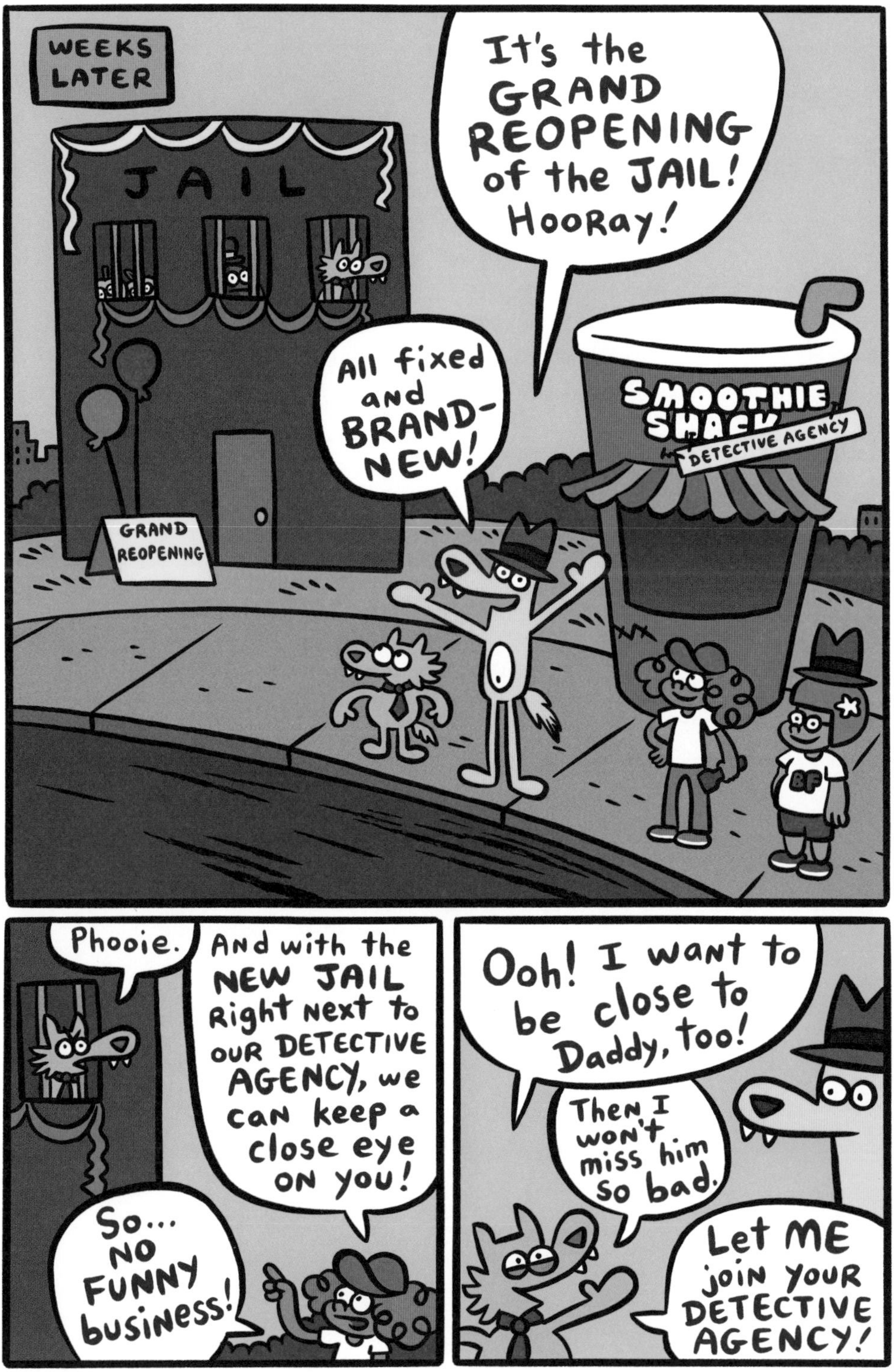
WEEKS LATER
JAIL
It's the GRAND REOPENING of the JAIL! Hooray!
All fixed and BRAND-NEW!
SMOOTHIE SHACK
DETECTIVE AGENCY
GRAND REOPENING
Phooie.
And with the NEW JAIL right next to our DETECTIVE AGENCY, we can keep a close eye on you!
So... NO FUNNY business!
Ooh! I want to be close to Daddy, too!
Then I won't miss him so bad.
Let ME join your DETECTIVE AGENCY!

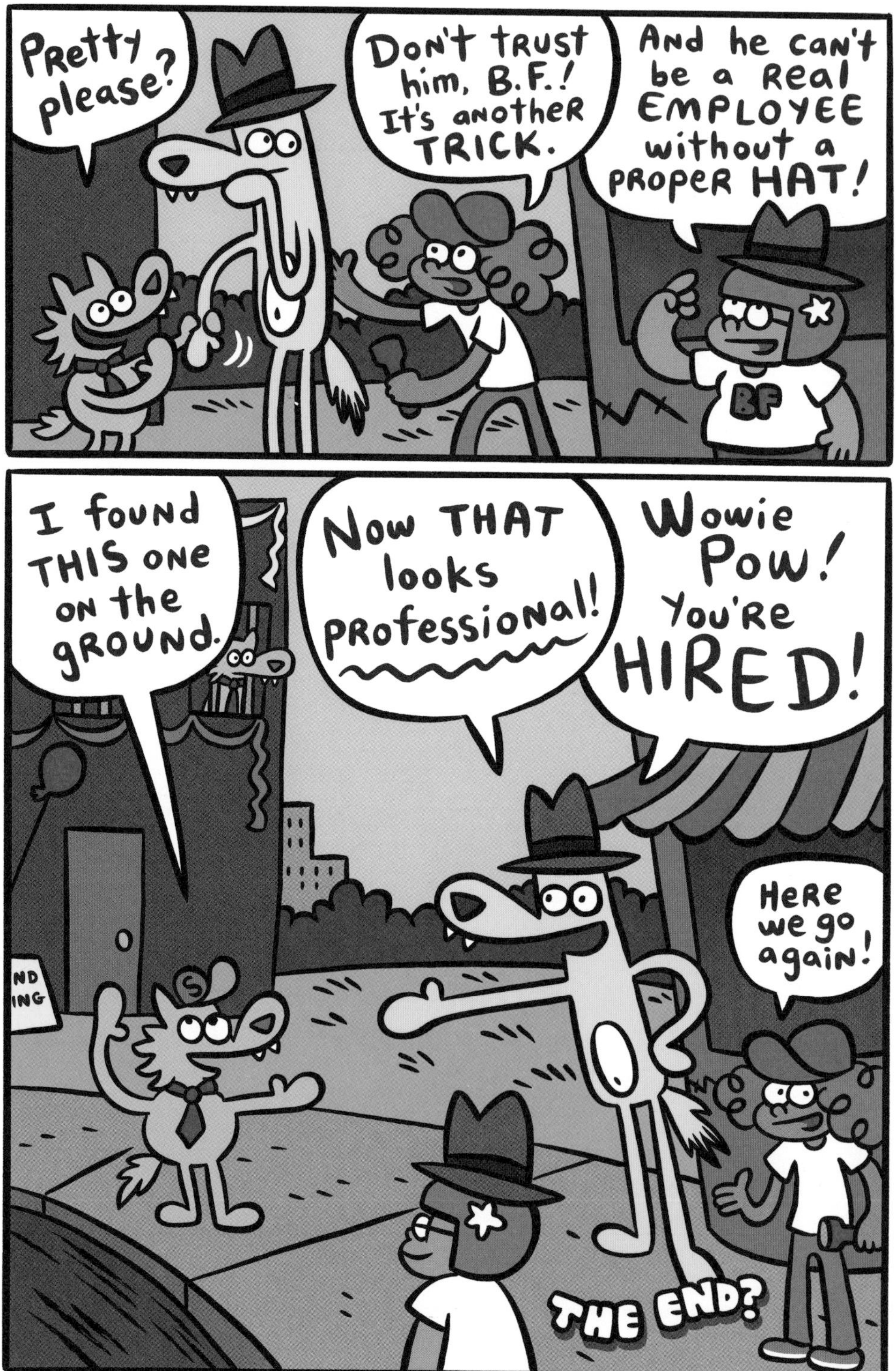
Pretty please?
Don't trust him, B.F.! It's another TRICK.
And he can't be a real EMPLOYEE without a proper HAT!
BF
I found THIS one on the ground.
Now THAT looks professional!
Wowie Pow! You're HIRED!
Here we go again!
THE END?

JAMES KOCHALKA

is one of the most unique and prolific cartoonists working in America today. His comics have been published internationally, and he's developed animated cartoons for Nickelodeon. Among his best-known work is the Johnny Boo series, for which he won an Eisner Award in 2019. In 2011, James became the first official Vermont Cartoonist Laureate. He and his wife, Amy, continue to live in Vermont, where they raised their family of two boys and too many cats.